THE ADVENTURES OF CATVINKLE

Pushkin Press
71–75 Shelton Street
London WC2H 9JQ

The Adventures of Catvinkle was first published by
Penguin Random House Australia in 2018

First published by Pushkin Children's Books in 2018

1 3 5 7 9 8 6 4 2

ISBN 13: 978-1-78269-174-7

Cover and internal illustrations by Laura Stitzel

Cover and internal design by Bruno Herfst
© Penguin Random House Australia

Printed and bound by CPI Group (UK) Ltd, Croydon CRO 4YY

www.pushkinpress.com

ELLIOT PERLMAN

THE ADVENTURES OF CATVINKLE

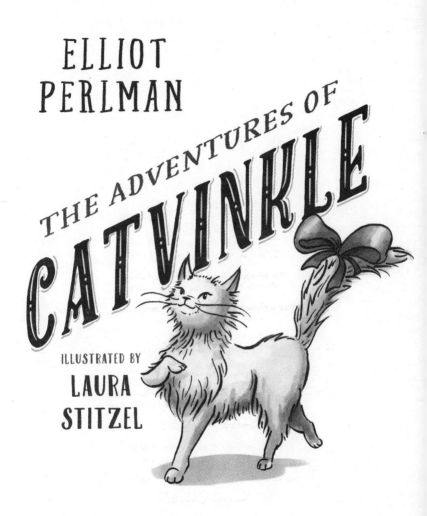

ILLUSTRATED BY
LAURA STITZEL

PUSHKIN CHILDREN'S

For Nicholas and Alexander

PART ONE

THE SURPRISE

CHAPTER 1

Once there was a barber who cut and styled the hair of men, women, children and babies. In fact, if you were at all human and had a head which had some hair, he could give you a very nice haircut.

The name of the barber was Mr Sabatini. He was a kind man and he liked to make people look as nice as he could. As you'll soon see, he liked animals too – although he didn't give them haircuts or even fur trims. But he was comfortable in a world of wet hair and even wet fur.

Mr Sabatini's barber salon was part of his house in Herring Street. Herring Street is a street in

Amsterdam, which is a big city in a country that has two names: Holland and The Netherlands. None of the animals in this story know why.

He lived there with a dear friend of his, a white cat known as Catvinkle who had long, strong, quite substantial whiskers that were almost as thick as wings. Mr Sabatini loved Catvinkle very much. In fact, he loved her so much that he bought her a large red bow. Catvinkle wore it proudly tied to the end of her tail, making her look like a walking furry birthday present that Mr Sabatini got to play with every day.

Catvinkle had her own room in Mr Sabatini's house, though she kindly allowed him to share it and use it as a study. She loved this room. It was slightly sunken below the ground, so that when Catvinkle would sit in the space in front of the window she could see feet and legs walking past her on Herring Street outside.

She found people's shoes, socks and legs endlessly fascinating. They all walked at different speeds. Sometimes Catvinkle noticed that people's

socks didn't match. This didn't happen often but you could be lucky every now and then.

Then there were the animal legs. Catvinkle could recognise many of the passing animals just by their paws. 'Gee, that Russian wolfhound is up early. I wonder where he has to go in such a hurry,' she might say to herself from the comfort of her basket.

Catvinkle's room had pleated curtains of cream and royal blue that went from above the window to the red carpeted floor. When Mr Sabatini closed them in the evenings they would sweep the floor like a ballgown flowing across a dance floor. There was an old desk with matching chair, both of shiny dark wood, a soft armchair in a creamy colour to match the curtains, and books lining the walls almost all the way along.

But Catvinkle's two favourite things in the room were the deep fireplace – where Mr Sabatini kept the fire going all through the damp and colder months – and her big comfy wicker basket. Catvinkle found it hard to imagine anything better than lying in her basket with the fire glowing to keep her coat warm and her water bowl just a paw's length away.

One morning, Mr Sabatini picked up Catvinkle's basket very gently as she was sleeping. He took it into his bathroom and placed it carefully beside the basin so that he could have his morning chat with Catvinkle while he shaved.

'Good morning, my dear Catvinkle.'

A little flick of the tail came from deep within the basket, which was Catvinkle's way of saying good morning. She always did this and it always made him smile.

'It looks like you're having a lovely warm and snuggy sleep, Catvinkle,' said Mr Sabatini. He had shaving cream all over the bottom half of his face and his razor blade was scraping it away.

Another little flick of the tail came from Catvinkle, which he took to mean, 'Yes, it is a lovely sleep!'

'So I guess you don't want to come out with me for a quick breakfast?'

The third flick of her tail meant that she agreed. She was too warm and snuggy to leave her basket.

This little exchange was part of their morning routine. Mr Sabatini always asked Catvinkle if she'd like to come for a breakfast walk, and Catvinkle always politely declined with a little flick of her tail. They enjoyed being polite to each other. Mr Sabatini was a very polite barber, and Catvinkle was for the most part a very polite cat. At least, she was polite to Mr Sabatini and his clients.

'Of course, dear Catvinkle. You get some more sleep,' said Mr Sabatini. He washed and dried his face so that now it was not only smooth but clean.

Then he gently picked up Catvinkle in her basket, took the basket from the bathroom and placed it down on the floor back in her own room. Her water bowl was full and the fire in the fireplace was crackling. Catvinkle was in heaven.

Mr Sabatini put on his coat to go out for his daily breakfast of coffee, wholemeal bread and *appelstroop*. He loved going for his quick morning walks because he found his city so beautiful. Whenever he walked along the canals, fresh air brushing against his face, he never failed to enjoy looking at the wonderful old narrow brick houses. Each was a different colour, nestled cosily against its neighbour, and each was full of stories that came from all the people who had lived there over hundreds of years. Mr Sabatini thought he had to be one of the luckiest barbers in the whole world to live in such a place.

Not only was his city beautiful, but interesting things were always popping up. You just had to be ready to see them. This morning, for example, as he was enjoying the feel of the cobblestones under his feet, he saw a Russian wolfhound going for a walk with another animal that looked like no dog he'd ever seen. It looked more like . . . a llama?

Mr Sabatini rubbed his eyes to make sure he was awake. Could it really be a llama, not in Peru but here in central Amsterdam? The llama was walking sleepily and seemed to be about to fall into the canal when the Russian wolfhound lengthened his neck to get slightly ahead of the llama and guided it to safety with his snout. This is the kind of lovely unexpected thing Mr Sabatini would see when he went for his walks, the kind of thing that made him even happier. What a helpful dog that Russian wolfhound was, Mr Sabatini thought to himself. He had really stuck his neck out for that llama.

Kindness in people and in animals made Mr Sabatini feel warm inside. What would his own animal friend, Catvinkle, have done in the same circumstance, he wondered. Would Catvinkle help other animals? She does seem to spend a lot of time on her own, he thought, although perhaps she goes out when he's busy washing, styling and cutting people's hair. Of course, there's nothing wrong with spending time on your own. But perhaps she needs a friend, Mr Sabatini wondered to himself as he went inside his favourite local cafe.

Mr Sabatini didn't have time to stay for very long this morning. He was in a bit of a hurry because a lady and two children were coming in for a haircut and he didn't want to be late home. He quickly ate his wholemeal bread and *appelstroop* in the cafe, and he was walking home drinking his coffee in a takeaway cup when he saw a beautiful white dog with black spots, a Dalmatian. The dog shyly came up to him.

Mr Sabatini bent down to give the Dalmatian a quick, friendly pat. What a lovely dog, he thought. As he was patting her he read her name, 'Ula', on the dog tag that was attached to her red leather collar. He noticed, too, that Ula's big brown eyes were a little sad, and that the fur on her coat was not sitting entirely smoothly. Some of her fur stood up from the rest of her coat. Being a barber he would notice a thing like this. He looked around to see if there were any humans nearby who might be connected to Ula. No, there didn't seem to be anyone.

So, with his coffee in one hand, he stayed down on one knee and gently patted Ula. He looked carefully in her eyes as he spoke. 'Don't you have anywhere to stay, Ula?'

Ula leaned into his leg and nuzzled it with her nose. Mr Sabatini understood that to mean that he was right, that she didn't have anywhere to stay.

She had such a kind face with her big brown eyes that Mr Sabatini wanted to spend more time patting Ula.

But he was torn because he was in a hurry.

What could he do? If he spent too much more time patting Ula he would be late.

'Well,' said Mr Sabatini, 'I have to get back to my salon to cut some people's hair, but why don't you come along with me? I can give you a drink of water and you can get warm inside.'

So Mr Sabatini and Ula walked back to his home. When they got there, Mr Sabatini saw that the lady and the two children were just arriving for their haircuts. He wasn't late, thankfully, but he didn't want to keep them waiting, so he asked them to come into the salon while he showed his new friend, Ula, where she could get some water.

Mr Sabatini went downstairs to the room where Catvinkle slept and opened the door.

'Ula,' he said, 'I'd like you to meet Catvinkle. I'm sure she'll be happy to share some of her water with you.'

CHAPTER 2

Catvinkle was in shock. One moment earlier she had been peacefully napping by the fire in her own room. Now, suddenly, there was a spotted dog standing by the door, and Mr Sabatini had gone upstairs.

A dog!

Ula, for her part, was very uncomfortable being in a cat's room. And not the room of just any cat. This cat had a beautiful white shiny coat of fur, impressive thick white whiskers, slinky paws and a big red bow tied around her tail. Ula wasn't looking to make trouble.

'Hello, Catvinkle. My name is Ula, although many people call me "Wet Ula".'

Catvinkle didn't say anything. Instead she just stared at Ula from her wicker basket. Was she asleep and still dreaming? She dipped her paw into her water bowl and trickled a little water onto her face. Yes, she was definitely awake, and yes, there was really a dog in her room. A dog!

'*Oo-la?*' asked the still sleepy cat.

'No, it's *U-la*, like You-la, rhymes with *school-la* or *ruler*,' said Ula.

'Wouldn't that be You-*ler*?' asked Catvinkle.

'No, not in my case. Anyway, sadly, I often get called Wet Ula,' said the spotty dog.

'Did you say Wet Ula?'

'Yes,' said Ula.

'Why are you called *that*?' Catvinkle asked.

She was shocked to be having a conversation with a dog and in her own room. This was horrible. She couldn't believe that Mr Sabatini, who was such a kind man, had brought a dog in here. Perhaps this Ula creature wasn't really a dog. Perhaps she just *looked* like a dog.

'Do you mean why am I called *Wet* or why am

I called Ula?' Ula was trying to be polite to the suspicious cat.

'Let's start with *Wet*. *Are* you wet?' asked Catvinkle.

'Not right now, not as far as I can tell. But sometimes when I'm cold I can't tell if I'm also wet. I'm a bit cold now but I'm sure that lovely warm fire will warm me up in no time. Does that ever happen to you, that when you're cold you think you might also be wet?'

'Well,' said Catvinkle, stretching, 'as you can see, I have a lovely warm fire in my very own room.' She scratched her neck casually with a rear paw as she continued. 'A fire in my very own room in this house where I live with Mr Sabatini. So I'm not cold very often.'

'I see,' said Ula.

Ula slid her right front paw very quietly and slowly towards the fire, closely followed by her left front paw.

'So you're never so cold that you think you might also be wet?' she asked Catvinkle.

'*Sometimes* I am,' said Catvinkle, 'when I'm in the sky.'

'In the sky?' said Ula with great surprise. 'What do you mean?'

'Never mind what I mean,' said Catvinkle, a little snippily.

Ula was worried that Catvinkle might notice her attempts to creep closer to the fire, but she was so chilly that she had to take the chance.

'Cough,' she said and, as she did, she raised her tummy off the ground and inched herself just that tiny bit closer to the fire. 'Cough, cough.' She inched her tummy forward again.

'You're not sick, are you?' Catvinkle asked, more out of suspicion than friendly concern.

'Er, no,' said Ula.

'You haven't explained why you're called *Wet* Ula, or why you're trying to use up my fire to dry off or why you're in my room. You haven't explained anything,' said the frustrated Catvinkle, who still could not believe she had woken to find a dog in her otherwise perfect room.

'I didn't mean to use up your fire. Aren't you getting the same warmth from the fire that you got before I came in? I didn't realise fires couldn't be shared. Do you want me to explain why I'm called "Wet" Ula?'

'Yes, I do,' said Catvinkle. 'But before you try to explain anything else or use up any more of the warmth from my fire, the fire in *my* room in *my* house, the one I share with *my* dear friend Mr Sabatini, whom I've known for a very long time and didn't just meet this morning –'

'Yes, what is it?' asked Ula.

'Well,' said Catvinkle, 'I really do think you need to clear up one thing first, because I'm not sure if I'm awake or dreaming. You look to me a lot like – well, there's no other way of putting this – a dog. Wet or not, are you . . . a *dog*?'

'Yes, I'm a Dalmatian. We're *all* dogs, us Dalmatians.'

'Did you *tell* Mr Sabatini that you're a dog?' asked the bewildered Catvinkle.

'I didn't have to tell him. He knew I was a dog. Just look at me.'

'But . . . he likes *cats*,' Catvinkle said. 'How do you know he knew you were a dog?'

'Well, he let me rub my nose against his leg and he patted me,' Ula answered.

'*I* rub *my* nose against his leg and *I* get pats from him,' Catvinkle protested. 'Do *I* look like a dog to you?'

'No, you look like a cat to me – and a most elegant one, if I might say,' said Ula diplomatically.

'Well, I *am* a cat, a most elegant cat, and yes, you *can* say that if you feel you want to.'

'Maybe Mr Sabatini likes to pat dogs as well as cats?' Ula suggested.

'First I've heard of it,' said Catvinkle dismissively. 'Never before have I seen him pat a dog, no one has ever told me that they have seen him pat a dog, and then one morning I'm rudely awakened from a beautiful snuggy nap by a wet dog!'

'Oh, I'm not actually wet, remember?' said Ula in an attempt to make Catvinkle feel better.

'But didn't you say your name was *Wet* Something-or-other?' asked Catvinkle.

'Wet Ula, yes. But my parents named me Ula. The "Wet" part I've sort of picked up along the way,' Ula said sadly.

'Picked up along the way? What does that mean?' asked Catvinkle, more confused than ever.

CHAPTER 3

So Ula began to tell Catvinkle the story of how she became known as 'Wet'. She didn't mind telling the story because it meant that she could stay near the fire.

She had been living with some nice people in a nice house when they decided to have the rooms in their house painted before selling the house and moving away to a new town. The people wanted the house to stay warm to help the paint dry in the rooms, so they closed all the windows and all the doors and were in the process of moving out to a hotel before leaving for the new town.

They were so busy packing up all their things, putting them into boxes, moving the boxes into a van on the street and locking up the house that they didn't realise that Ula was not where they thought she was. Each one of the family members thought Ula was with another member of the family.

No one had noticed that Ula had gone out walking. In fact, at the very moment the van drove away with all their things, no one was thinking about Ula at all. They were too concerned with whether their many boxes would fit into the van. Ula had been on her way back from visiting her friends at her club, Puppies Anonymous.

'I would have been back sooner,' Ula explained to Catvinkle, 'but there was a big scary grey dog that kept chasing me every time I got close to the house. So I had to wait till he went away. Perhaps you know this dog?'

'What's Puppies Anonymous?' asked Catvinkle, ignoring Ula's question.

'Puppies Anonymous is a special friendship club for dogs and puppies who have lost their name tags or else who just want to take a break from being some-one's pet for a while. It's a place dogs can go and let their fur down, slip off their collars if they can, and chew the fat – or else gnaw on a nice bone. It's on the eastern side of Vondelpark,' Ula explained.

'Are you a member of Puppies Anonymous?' asked Catvinkle.

'Yes,' answered Ula.

'Gee,' said Catvinkle, surprised, 'we cats have a club called Kittens Anonymous and *I'm* a member of that. It's on the western side of Vondelpark. We were going to make it on the eastern side of Vondelpark but we'd heard that whole area had gone to the dogs.'

'So anyway, back to me being called "Wet",' continued Ula. 'When I finally came back from Puppies Anonymous to the freshly painted house after running away and hiding from the big scary grey dog, the nice people who lived there had gone. I found a note they had left for the newspaper boy saying goodbye to him and telling him that they were moving first to a hotel and then to another city.

'There was no one there to let me back in and no one to tell me where their hotel was. I thought that they must have chosen a hotel that welcomes

nice, clean, well-behaved dogs. So I went walking in
search of that hotel. On the way, though, it started to
rain and my coat got all wet. I went to the first hotel
I could find to look for my human friends and the
man at the desk said, "This dog smells like a *wet* dog!
People won't want to stay in a hotel that smells of wet
dog." Then he read my name on my dog tag attached
to my collar and said, "Out you go, Wet Ula!"

'So I went into the next hotel and a woman at the front desk there said, "Ooh! You smell like wet dog. Out you go, Wet Ula!" In every hotel I went to, the person at the front desk said, "No wet dogs allowed. Out you go, Wet Ula!"

'Just when my coat was finally completely dry, it started to rain and I got wet all over again. And now I can't seem to get rid of the smell of wet fur,

even on dry days. I keep walking and walking, looking for a place to stay, but it seems *nobody* likes the smell of wet dog. And now everybody calls me "Wet Ula".'

'What about the people you used to live with in the house that got painted? Where are they now?' Catvinkle asked.

'By now they will have moved into their new house in a new town. I don't know how to find them or if I'll ever see them again,' said Ula. She looked sad.

'I see,' said Catvinkle, her paws all warm and toasty from the fire, her tail casually curling and uncurling in the air behind her. 'This *is* a sad story, I must admit. Not even a dog deserves to have a story like this, probably.'

'Thank you,' said Ula.

'But what does any of this have to do with me? Whether you are wet or not, why are you here in my room?' asked Catvinkle.

It was a good question and it led to something strange happening. Ula did something many of us do. She said something she *thought* was true even though it was not true. She said, 'Mr Sabatini told me I could come home with him and stay in his house . . . forever.'

Mr Sabatini had not said this, so why did Ula tell Catvinkle he had? Ula *wanted* Mr Sabatini to have said this *so very much* that in her mind she had convinced herself that he really had said it.

Catvinkle's ears pricked up on her head like two furry sails on a furry sailboat. She was very disturbed to hear this. How could Mr Sabatini have invited a dog to live with them? Surely it was not true.

'Are you sure Mr Sabatini said this?' Catvinkle asked.

'Oh yes,' answered Ula, without being able to look Catvinkle in the eye because she really wasn't sure at all. 'I heard him with my own ears – which, though floppy, are excellent for hearing things like this.'

'Are you sure it wasn't *another* barber speaking to *another* animal about this *other* barber's house?' asked Catvinkle hopefully.

'No, it was Mr Sabatini,' said Ula.

'Are you sure he wasn't talking to a *cat* that might have been near you at the time?'

'No, there were no cats around at the time,' said Ula.

'Well, that might be because cats and dogs don't get on,' suggested Catvinkle snippily.

'That's possible,' said Ula.

Catvinkle then slowly asked Ula a question that had come to her all of a sudden, but took a moment longer than usual to say. 'Did Mr Sabatini tell you the *other* thing about any animals who ever live here?'

'What *other* thing?' asked Ula.

'The other thing he might have forgotten to tell you because he was running late for his next haircut appointment is that the only animals who can live here with him and me are ones I *say* can live here. Did he tell you that?'

'No, he didn't say that. How many other animals live here other than you?' asked Ula.

'Other than me, let me see,' said Catvinkle, thinking. 'Other than me, *no* other animals live here. Not one. Are you good at counting? If not,

I can help you. If you had one other animal living here and you *minused* that one – that is, if you took it away and made it go walking back to the house that was being painted or wherever it came from – you'd have none. Which is exactly the number of other animals that live here with Mr Sabatini and me. None!'

There was only one problem with Catvinkle telling Ula that Mr Sabatini had said that Catvinkle could choose which animals could live with them. It wasn't true. Catvinkle wanted Mr Sabatini to have said this *so very much* that in her mind she had convinced herself that he really had said it. They had each told each other something that wasn't true, believing it to be true simply because they *wanted* it to be true.

'How many animals have wanted to come and live with you and Mr Sabatini?' asked Ula.

'Lots,' said Catvinkle. 'More than I can count on one paw.'

'How many can you count on one paw?' asked Ula.

'As many as I like. It's *my* paw. I can use it

again and again for counting. I've got three others, you know.'

'So no other animal has ever been allowed to live here with you and Mr Sabatini?' Ula asked sadly.

'There simply isn't the room. Mr Sabatini likes his space. It's been that way ever since he first patted me as a tiny kitten and said, "I must have that little Catvinkle live with me forever."'

CHAPTER 4

Ula looked around the room, trying to find something that might distract Catvinkle from telling Ula she would have to leave. Ula really wanted to stay in front of the fire at least a little longer. What could she talk about?

She noticed a pair of tiny baby shoes lying on the floor near Catvinkle's basket. They were crocheted light blue, with a dark blue zig-zag pattern and one brown button on each shoe the colour of a tortoise's shell.

'Are they baby shoes? They sure are beautiful,' Ula said.

As Catvinkle took her eyes off Ula to look at the baby shoes, the cold dog took the opportunity to move her whole body again just a bit closer to the fire.

'Yes, they are beautiful,' said Catvinkle with pride. 'But they're not really baby shoes, they're *my* shoes.'

'I've seen babies wearing shoes just like that,' said Ula.

'Well, yes, a baby came in with his mother to have his first haircut. Mr Sabatini gave the baby boy just one snip for the haircut but that was all the time the baby needed to decide he wanted me to have his shoes. You see, he patted me and I even let him touch my whiskers, and he was so grateful that he gave me his baby shoes.'

'Could he talk, this baby?' asked Ula.

'No, not really. He was just a tiny baby.'

'Then how do you know he wanted you to have his baby shoes?'

'Well,' answered Catvinkle, 'he left them behind for me.'

'Maybe they fell off and his mother didn't notice and they left them here by mistake?' suggested Ula.

'No, no, that's not what happened at all!'

'But how do you know?'

'There are a few ways that I know he wanted me to have them,' Catvinkle said. 'First, while Mr Sabatini made his mother's hair look all soft, shiny and manageable after he'd finished the baby boy's haircut, the baby boy pushed one of his shoes towards me with his nose.'

'I'm trying to picture it,' said Ula. 'Do you mean he was crawling on his tummy like this?' Ula crawled on her tummy towards the fire. 'Or,' Ula continued, 'was he crawling on his knees more like this?' Then Ula crawled on her knees closer and closer to the warmth of the fire.

'Well,' said Catvinkle, 'let's see now. From memory, it was a crawl with a bit of tummy and a bit of knees – or elbows, I should say, since he was a baby human. Then he pushed one of his shoes towards me with his nose. Please don't try to act that out. I wouldn't want you to burn your snout by getting too close to the fire.'

'Sorry,' said Ula.

'So then I thanked the baby and he blew a bubble out of his mouth which, if you know anything about human babies, was his way of saying, "You're welcome, Catvinkle. They'll look great on you. Wear them in good health!" Do you know anything about baby humans?'

'A little,' said Ula.

'A little, how lovely. Sounds like I know more. So then I said to him, "Baby boy, are you sure you want me to have them? If you don't really want me to have these beautiful blue baby shoes forever, hop up and down on one leg. But if you think that you're going to grow out of them and that they'd get much better use from me, do anything else but don't hop up and down on one leg." And guess what? He just lay there on his tummy looking at the floor.'

'He didn't hop?'

'Not one hop.'

'Had he learned to walk yet?'

'He didn't say. But however you look at it, they're clearly my baby shoes. I think I've proven it beyond a shadow of a doubt,' said Catvinkle.

'I see,' said Ula. 'But what exactly do you do with baby shoes?'

Catvinkle jumped up out of her basket and her tail stood tall, pointing to the ceiling. 'I can't tell you that!'

'Why not?' Ula said, surprised at the cat's prickly reaction.

'It's one of my secrets,' said Catvinkle. Ula's question had Catvinkle up and moving like nothing else had. She was now out of her basket and swinging both front paws from right to left as though doing some strange sort of exercise.

'*One* of your secrets!' said Ula. 'How many secrets do you have?'

'I'm not sure if I should tell you that either.'

Catvinkle continued with her exercises. Ula watched as the cat tried a different stretch. She was standing on her hind paws like a human walking on legs, her top paws in the air. Ula wanted to ask her what she was doing but she was still trying to learn all she could about Catvinkle's secrets.

'Why can't you tell me how many secrets you have? Is it a secret?'

'It used to be, but I told a certain kitten at Kittens Anonymous and now all the cats there know.'

'Do you talk about your secrets at Kittens Anonymous?'

'Oh yes, all the time. There's no point having secrets unless some cats know and other cats don't. All the cats who don't know *want* to know and all the cats who *do* know are constantly in danger of telling the cats who *don't* know. We have a lot of fun at Kittens Anonymous telling and not telling each other's secrets.'

'Do any dogs know your secrets?'

'I don't *know* any dogs.'

'Then you could tell me safely because cats don't talk to me on account of how I'm a dog.'

Ula was very interested in secrets, because dogs didn't often have secrets – and if they ever did, they tended to lose them quite quickly. Once, Ula had found a big juicy bone on her way to Puppies Anonymous. She knew that if the other dogs found out about the bone they'd want her to share it, or they'd even want to take it from her and have it all to themselves. So she buried it in the park. The trouble was, she was so excited about the bone that she couldn't stop thinking about it. So when her friends had asked her how she was, she said with much excitement, 'I'm great! I just found a big juicy bone and I've hidden it over there!'

Ula remembered that bone fondly for a moment in silence and then continued. 'You've never told your secrets to a dog before. You might find the suspense exciting. Will I tell other dogs your secrets or will I keep them a secret from everyone? Just a thought.'

'Hmmm . . . I'm not sure,' Catvinkle said. 'To tell you my secrets I would have to trust you and know that you're very special.'

'Well, I *am* very special. I can sit, fetch, come when my name is called, lay down, beg and heel.'

'What's heel?'

'I was hoping you wouldn't ask me that. I've forgotten. Not much call for it these days.'

Now Catvinkle thought for a moment. 'Well, I suppose if I *did* tell you about a secret, you wouldn't tell any cats, because they wouldn't be caught dead talking to a dog. No offence.'

'None taken,' Ula replied, and waited eagerly to hear more.

CHAPTER 5

'Here goes!' said Catvinkle. 'I have three secrets. I'll tell you the first one and see how it feels. If it feels good to get it out of my fur I'll tell you another one. But if it doesn't feel good, I'd just as soon forget that I ever tried telling a secret to a dog.'

'Sounds fair,' said Ula.

'Ready?' asked Catvinkle.

'Do you mind if I come a bit closer to the fire first? I find it easier to keep a secret when I'm warm,' asked Ula.

Catvinkle nodded her agreement. 'I suppose that would be all right.'

Ula crept closer to the fire. She wanted to creep

even closer still, but thought that if she went too far in any one movement Catvinkle might change her mind about everything. She might even ask her to leave.

It sure was a beautiful room Catvinkle had. The fire was crackling and there were so many books in the bookshelves lining the walls. Ula looked around her, imagining a story in each of the books. So many stories, she thought. With this many stories a dog would never feel lonely or alone. A dog would never be bored. Then she remembered that she was in the middle of a story right now. It was a story about Catvinkle's secrets and she was just about to hear the first one.

'Okay,' said Catvinkle, 'here's the first of my three secrets.' She took a deep breath then let it out. 'Secret number one *is* . . . I really only have two secrets.'

'Wow!' said Ula. 'I never would have guessed that. You really only have two secrets!'

'Shhh!' hissed Catvinkle. 'Do you want the whole world to know?'

'No, I don't *think* so,' said Ula.

'You don't think so!' cried Catvinkle.

'Well, I've never really thought about it,' said Ula in her own defence.

'If you want to know the other two secrets the right answer is, "No, I don't want the whole world to know that you've really only got two secrets."'

'Okay, I *don't* want the whole world to know you've only got two secrets,' said Ula.

'Good. Now, secret number two is . . . I am a baby-shoe dancer.'

'Oh my goodness!' said Ula. 'That's incredible! I can't believe it!' She paused. 'Is that a good response?'

'Yes, that's pretty good,' said Catvinkle, impressed.

'Just one thing,' said Ula. 'What's a baby-shoe dancer?'

'In the world of cats and kittens,' explained Catvinkle, 'when we're alone and no people or other animals are watching us, we like to dance. And the most popular dance among cats and kittens is baby-shoe dancing. That is probably why that dear little baby boy gave me his shoes. I think he knew.'

'I see,' said Ula.

Catvinkle continued. 'Two years ago I won the National Kitten Baby-Shoe Dancing Competition. Last year I came second to a stupid show-off cat named Twinkiepaws.'

'Twinkiepaws!' exclaimed Ula.

'You know her?' asked Catvinkle.

'No, it's just a very unusual name.'

'It's a dumb name for a dumb cat. I heard a rumour that it's not even her real name. No, her real name is *Spinnenkop*. Twinkiepaws indeed! That's just her baby-shoe dancing competition name. She's so . . . *happy* with herself, ugh! I got tired of her boasting about how good at baby-shoe dancing she is. That's when I decided I should learn. It took some time and a lot of practice but now I'm pretty good at it. I'm ready to challenge that show-offy cat again this year and teach her that she's not so good after all. Did you know she gets her tail fur puffed up and fluffed up before the competition?'

'I can just imagine,' said Ula. She knew it wasn't very nice to gossip, but she was finding that listening innocently to someone *else* gossip, especially if you were relaxed and warm in front of the fire, was extremely pleasant.

'No, Twinkiepaws is even worse than you might be imagining. She's a show-off with an unnaturally fluffy tail and I hate her!'

'Hate's a very strong word,' said Ula.

'I know, but I can't think of a better one to describe the way I feel about Twinkiepaws.'

Catvinkle had got herself all fired up in describing her dislike of her baby-shoe dancing rival. In fact, she was so worked up that, without realising, she was walking around on two feet like a human.

'Wow, you're standing on two paws,' said Ula in admiration. 'Standing *and* walking!'

'Yes,' said Catvinkle, 'I have to. It's part of my training for the National Kitten Baby-Shoe Dancing Competition. Did I mention that it's only two days away? I'm going to win back my title from Twinkiepaws. Then, when I do, I'm going to prance, march and strut into the centre of town to the market and all the cats in town, including the

visiting tourist cats, will see me. Every cat will be in the market on the first day of herring season.'

'Is that a special day?' asked Ula.

'Is it special?! What planet do you live on? It's the most special day of the year, other than perhaps my birthday,' answered Catvinkle.

'That's news to a dog. But, Catvinkle, I have a

question. You said your second secret is that you're a baby-shoe dancer.'

'Yes, I know I said that. I was there when I said it,' said Catvinkle.

'Well,' said Ula, 'if other cats and kittens have seen you do your baby-shoe dancing, then they will know that this is a type of dance that you like to do.'

'I don't just *like* doing it, I'm very good at doing it. Excellent, really. Sorry, what was the question?'

'Well, if these other cats and kittens at Kittens Anonymous have seen you baby-shoe dance, how can it be a secret?'

'Oh, I think I understand,' Catvinkle said. 'Maybe some cats know and others have forgotten, but no one else knows except some of them and now you.'

Ula moved her head from side to side, suggesting she really was having trouble understanding.

'Look, Ula,' Catvinkle went on, 'here's the secret to secrets: they belong to you, or in this case to me. It's up to *me* to decide what is a secret and what isn't. A long time ago I decided that my baby-shoe dancing was one of my secrets. So it's a secret. Okay! It's as simple as that.'

'So it doesn't matter how many cats know?' asked Ula.

'Yes, of course it matters how many cats know!' said Catvinkle, getting a tiny bit frustrated with the wide-eyed dog before her.

'I don't get it,' said Ula.

'I can't be expected to make perfect sense all the time. Get it, *purr-fect* sense?!'

'I don't get it,' said Ula again.

'It's a cat joke. I've got to remember that one. Next question, please,' said Catvinkle.

Ula perked up, and her tail started wagging to and fro in time with her heartbeat at the idea of asking another question. 'What does baby-shoe dancing look like? Would you do some baby-shoe dancing for me?'

'But I've only just met you. And, anyway, you're a dog,' said Catvinkle.

'Yes, I am a dog, but dogs are really great.'

'Look, Ula, you see these paws, these whiskers and this tail? I'm a cat. I'm never going to agree with you about that. I can't!' said Catvinkle, standing on her two bottom paws with her tail swishing about behind her.

Ula thought for a moment. 'What if you practised your baby-shoe dancing and I just happened to be here?' she suggested.

'Well, I *do* have to practise. But you'd have to promise two things: that you won't tell anyone, and that you accept that I'm not dancing for you. I need to practise my routine so I can beat Twinkiepaws, and you just happen to be here in the room.'

'Okay, I could promise that.'

Catvinkle put one of her bottom paws in the right baby shoe and one of her bottom paws in the left. With her eyes closed, Catvinkle counted softly to herself, 'One, two, three,' and began to dance. She swung her rump to the left and then to the right and back again, with her tail going the opposite way. Then she did a backflip in one direction and then another in the opposite direction.

'Wow!' said Ula.

CHAPTER 6

Both Catvinkle and Ula were so absorbed in Catvinkle's dancing that they didn't hear the sound of Mr Sabatini's footsteps getting closer and closer until suddenly the half-closed door burst open.

Catvinkle was so surprised when the door hit her in the tail that she jumped up high in the air. Mr Sabatini stood in the doorway, expecting to see both Catvinkle and his new friend, Ula, but he saw only Ula.

'Where is Catvinkle?' Mr Sabatini asked. But before Ula could try to say anything, he added, 'Oh, she must have gone out. I just wanted to see that you hadn't run out of water. I'll come back later. I have to give Anja and Ferdi their haircuts. They're visiting with their aunt. I've finished doing her hair, and now it's the children's turn. I'll come back and check in on you later.'

And with that he left. Ula trotted around to look behind the door. She thought she'd seen something quite extraordinary when Catvinkle had leapt into the air. She looked up towards the ceiling and there was Catvinkle, high up in the air, hovering in one spot. Ula could hardly believe her eyes. Catvinkle had her front paws tucked in under her, the bottom paws dangling like the legs of a human, and her tail was going round and round, with the bow at the tip of her tail spinning.

'What are you doing up there?'

'I got a fright,' said Catvinkle, 'and I jumped.'

'But how do you get so high? And how do you manage to stay there?'

'That's secret number three,' said Catvinkle, who felt as though she had been caught and forced to give up what was perhaps her most important secret. 'I can fly,' she said, trying to make it sound like the most normal thing in the world for a cat to say.

Ula was so surprised to see Catvinkle hovering above her that she dropped to her tummy on the floor, arching her back and stretching out her front paws so that she made the shape of the letter 'U'.

'You can fly?!' she exclaimed.

'But I can't stay up forever,' said the flying Catvinkle.

Catvinkle's fluffy tail was spinning very fast, faster and faster, round and round like a merry-go-round that was out of control. The red bow on Catvinkle's tail spun like the propeller on a helicopter, blowing air around the room. Ula could not believe her eyes.

'I get tired if I do this for long. In fact, I'm getting tired now,' said Catvinkle. 'Oh no! I think I'm going to f-a-a-all.'

And with that, Catvinkle fell right on top of Ula and her face came to rest buried in Ula's fur.

Ula didn't know what to think. On the one paw, it was a shock to have someone suddenly fall on your back, especially if that someone was a cat.

On another paw, it felt quite good to have something nice and warm to take the chill off your fur, a bit like a blanket, a furry one that was breathing.

There were still two more paws to consider. On the one back paw, it felt like a massage or at least a very good pat to have the claws of the out-of-breath cat kneading on top of Ula's back so as not to fall off and onto the floor.

With one last paw to consider how she felt to have this cat fall from the ceiling on top of her, Ula realised it was scary to think that the cat might complain about the smell of wet dog, just like the humans in the hotels had complained.

'What's that smell?' Catvinkle asked.

'Oh no, you're probably going to say I smell wet and that you hate the smell of wet dog,' said Ula. 'Go ahead, you might as well. Everybody says it.'

'No, not at all! It's all . . . musky. It's like a beautiful musky . . . mmm! I feel so calm and relaxed breathing in this musky smell.'

Catvinkle buried her nose into Ula's fur. 'I *love* this smell! It's the best smell I've ever smelled. Is that how you always smell?'

'I think so,' said Ula. 'I'm not really sure because to me I don't smell like anything.'

Catvinkle had smelled some good smells in her time – the hyacinths in Vondelpark, the herring at Friend's Herring Shop on the first day of herring season, sour milk that's been left in the sun and, of course, old socks – but this unexpected musky dog smell was a life-changing smell. She never would have imagined that she would sit calmly and happily on the back of a dog. But here she was on the back of a dog and she didn't want to move.

'Oh no, you *do* have a smell. And it's wonderful.' Catvinkle balanced herself so she was sitting right in the centre of Ula's back. She had been warned about dogs all her life. The cats she knew said terrible things about dogs. But if a dog could smell *that* good, how bad could they be? This dog didn't seem so bad at all.

'I think we should get to know each other even more than we already do. You and your musk have to stay right here!' said Catvinkle.

Catvinkle was still lying on top of Ula, breathing in the musky scent from her coat of fur when Ula asked if she would mind if she had a drink from Catvinkle's water bowl.

'What's that, dear musky-smelling dog? Did you say something? Some water? Yes, of course. You must consider my water bowl *your* water bowl,' said the blissed-out cat.

'Thank you, that's most kind of you,' said Ula.

She made her way awkwardly over to the water bowl with Catvinkle on her back. Usually she walked quite quickly with a happy little side-to-side swing. But this was careful, slow and steady, with Ula not wanting Catvinkle to think she was trying to tip her off. It was more the way an elephant would walk, a very old one.

'I wonder if I could ask you for two other things without you thinking me rude,' said Ula.

'Ask away, my musky canine friend.'

'Well, first, would you mind terribly taking a break from lying on my back?'

'Of course, Wet. Do you mind if I call you "Wet"?'

'Actually, I would prefer Ula.'

'Certainly, Ulee. Anything you say,' Catvinkle said, still in an almost dream-like state.

'And the other thing I was going to ask . . .' Ula hesitated.

'Anything, anything, if you'll promise to go on smelling like that,' said Catvinkle.

'But I don't know how I'm doing it,' explained Ula.

'No, neither do I, but don't go changing anything. Have you ever heard the expression "a leopard can't change its spots"?' Catvinkle asked.

'Yes.'

'Can a Dalmatian change her spots?' asked Catvinkle.

'No, I don't think so,' replied Ula.

'Fascinating, fascinating. I've always found Dalmatians to be one of the most fascinating and least objectionable dogs ever to come into my mind and sit there for a while.'

'You're really too kind,' said Ula. 'But would you like to hear the other thing I was going to ask you?'

'What? Oh yes, do go on, Ulee. What's the other thing?'

'Well,' said Ula, 'I'm so hungry. Do you think I could have something to eat?'

'Yes, of course. Where are my manners?' Catvinkle asked herself, still lying comfortably stretched out atop Ula's back.

'Under your basket?' Ula suggested.

'Follow me, Ulee. We'll go into the salon where Mr Sabatini is doing the children's hair. I know how to remind him to feed us. I tend not to actually speak to him with words. Perhaps I will one day, but the shock of my talking could cause him to faint and I wouldn't want that. I'm much too small to catch him if he fell – although I could *soften* his fall, I suppose. Anyway, not a word to anyone about my secrets. Okay?'

'You mean the baby-shoe dancing and the flying?'

'Yes, or the fact that I really only *have* two secrets.'

PART TWO

THE PLAN

CHAPTER 7

Catvinkle led Ula upstairs, where Mr Sabatini had just finished cutting the children's hair. The children were sitting next to each other in the hallway, swinging their legs, looking bored and maybe even a little sad while their aunt talked to Mr Sabatini.

'The weather is so surprising for this time of year. I didn't expect it to start raining cats and dogs,' the aunt was saying, just as Catvinkle and Ula walked into the salon. The appearance of the cat and dog just at that moment made the children laugh.

'Well, that's quite an entrance,' said Mr Sabatini.

'I didn't know you had a dog, Mr Sabatini,' said Anja, the young girl.

'To tell you the truth, Anja, neither did I and neither did Catvinkle. We just met this morning and here we are. But you two *seem* to be getting on all right,' said Mr Sabatini, addressing his comments to both Catvinkle and Ula. At this Catvinkle meowed and rubbed the side of her body up against Mr Sabatini's leg.

'I think that means "yes", Mr Sabatini,' said Anja's brother, Ferdi.

'Or perhaps that she wants some food,' said Mr Sabatini.

Catvinkle was enjoying showing Ula around the salon. In fact, she realised to her own amazement that she really did want Ula to stay. Was it because of the musky smell? Yes, that was definitely a big part of it. But there was more to Catvinkle's decision to welcome the dog.

Much to Catvinkle's surprise, she found herself enjoying the company of this very polite Dalmatian. It was much better than being alone so much of the time. She imagined it might be fun to have a friend to play with inside the house.

Ula was a dog and this might cause problems for Catvinkle if other cats found out. But Catvinkle decided that in front of any nosy cats or kittens she could just pretend that living with this dog had been forced on her by her human. She could tell another cat, 'It wasn't my idea but Mr Sabatini wanted a dog so much that I finally said "yes". You have to give humans their own way every now and then, you know.'

Of course, the Dalmatian would have to be trained. Dogs weren't as naturally good as cats at living inside and with people. They don't always know when to shut up, she thought, as Ula put her snout to Catvinkle's ear.

'Food?' Ula coughed in what sounded to the humans like a little bark.

Catvinkle turned her neck around so she was facing Ula. 'I'm working on it,' she whispered.

Then she rubbed the top of her head against the lower part of Mr Sabatini's leg.

'Oh, I definitely know what *this* means!' Mr Sabatini said. 'Catvinkle is hungry, and I'm sure her new friend, Ula, is too.'

Mr Sabatini excused himself from the aunt for just long enough to go to the kitchen. He filled Catvinkle's bowl with delicious pink salmon caught in the sea only the day before. He put more in another bowl for Ula, saying to her, 'I'm sorry, Ula, I didn't know you were coming so I don't have anything especially for dogs. I hope you enjoy the salmon. Catvinkle thinks it's delicious, don't you?'

Again, Catvinkle rubbed the top of her head against the lower part of Mr Sabatini's leg to show that she did, indeed, think it extremely delicious.

'I'd better get back to the salon and redo the aunt's hair. She's changed her mind and now wants a beehive, and that can take a lot of time. I think Anja and Ferdi are keen to get home. I'd hoped their new haircuts would make them happier but I don't think the haircuts have helped very much. Perhaps you two could come and spend some time with the children, once you've finished your snack?'

Mr Sabatini left the kitchen and went back to the salon.

'A beehive! Who wears a beehive on their head? I've never heard of such a thing!' said Ula.

'You're quite right about that, Ulee,' Catvinkle agreed. 'Best not to think about someone putting a house for stinging insects on their head. Let's think about food instead.'

The two animals sniffed their bowls, Catvinkle with pleasure and Ula with suspicion.

'So this is salmon?' asked Ula.

'Yes,' said Catvinkle. 'It's not herring, which is my favourite, but this is one of my favourites. Mr Sabatini knows I like it so he gets it for me. He gives the fishermen haircuts and in return they deliver fresh fish. It's a marvellous situation for a cat to be in. Why don't you try some?'

Ula was very hungry, but she'd never eaten salmon before and was a bit frightened to try it.

'Do cats eat salmon a lot?' she asked Catvinkle.

'As much as we can,' answered Catvinkle. 'We *love* it.'

'Catvinkle?' Ula began.

Catvinkle was burying her face in the salmon as deeply as she could. 'Yes, Ulee,' came her salmon-coated voice from the bottom of her bowl.

'Catvinkle, do you think that if I eat the salmon I'll become . . .' Ula couldn't finish the question.

'Become what, Ulee?'

'Do you think I'll become . . . a bit like a cat?'

'I wish it were that simple,' answered Catvinkle. 'It would make things a lot easier if just by eating salmon we could turn you into a cat. Then I could take you out with me into the town. I could take you to Kittens Anonymous and you could even be my partner in the National Kitten Baby-Shoe Dancing Competition. I'm invited with a guest, you know.'

'But I like going to Puppies Anonymous,' said Ula.

'That's not a place for cats,' said Catvinkle, lifting her head just for a moment from the salmon and shaking it. 'It's full of dogs!'

'But I'm not a cat!' protested Ula.

'Sadly, no. But try the salmon anyway. You'll love it. Don't you like trying new things?'

'Not sure. I never *choose* to try new things but sometimes I just have to. Do you like trying new things?' asked Ula.

'Oh yes. Sometimes I'll take my water *before* my salmon and sometimes I'll take my water *after* my salmon. A couple of times – and this will blow your mind – I've *started* my salmon then had a few licks of water and then gone *back* to my salmon, licking the bowl clean with *both* sides of my tongue. Crazy, I know! But I'm that kind of cat. I live on the edge!'

'My goodness, you're so adventurous!' exclaimed Ula.

'What can I say?' said Catvinkle. 'I'm very lucky to lead such an interesting life. Are you going to eat that lovely pink salmon, Ulee? No pressure, but if you're not . . .'

For the first time ever, Ula put her snout into a bowl of salmon. Sniff, sniff, she went. Then she put her tongue on it, just a bit. Then a bit more. Then she took a little bite. Then she took a big bite. In fact, it was such a big bite that she cleaned her bowl of every bit of salmon right then and there. Catvinkle was amazed. She had never seen salmon disappear so quickly.

'Wow, Ulee, they can't even *swim* that fast!'

'It was delicious!' said Ula.

'I'm so glad you liked it. I think you're really going to enjoy living here,' Catvinkle said.

CHAPTER 8

Just then Ula's ears stood up. She thought she heard a sound outside the kitchen. 'What's that? It sounds like a child crying. Do you hear it?'

But Catvinkle had her mind on something else. 'Ulee, there's a little piece of salmon hanging from the end of your snout. Do you mind if I just lean in and . . .'

Before Catvinkle finished her own sentence, she found herself straining her neck to reach the tip of Ula's snout. She stuck out her tongue, scooped the tiny piece of hanging salmon onto it and gobbled it up.

After she had done this, both Catvinkle and Ula heard a very different sound. First Ula had heard crying. Now it sounded like two children laughing.

'Did you hear that?' Catvinkle asked Ula.

'Should we go and find out if they're okay?' asked Ula. 'I love human children,' she said excitedly.

'I love human children too. But before we go, there's one thing we need to agree on first.'

'What's that?' asked Ula.

'Sometimes the only way to find things out from humans is to talk to them. You can't sniff and be sniffed because their noses don't smell very well. They can't sniff tails. They don't even *have* tails, poor things. So you just have to talk to them. Are you willing to let them know we can talk?'

'How about this for an idea,' suggested Ula. 'We'll go and look and sniff the children and then we'll be able to tell if they're nice. If they are nice, we can let them know we can talk. What do you think, Catvinkle?'

'Good idea, Ulee.'

So they went out to investigate and sniff and they

found it was Anja and Ferdi, the two children who had come with their aunt to have their hair cut. The children were very happy to see them and took it in turns to pat Catvinkle and Ula. In fact, they patted Catvinkle and Ula so nicely that Catvinkle decided to speak to them.

'Were you crying?' asked Catvinkle.

'Ferdi was,' said Anja, and then she shook her head as though to wake herself up. Wait a minute! It sounded to her as though the cat with the thick white whiskers and the big red bow tied around her tail had just asked her a question.

'Ferdi, did you hear what I heard?' Anja asked.

'It sounded as if Catvinkle talked,' said Ferdi in amazement.

'I did! I did! You can ask Ula,' said Catvinkle.

'She really did,' said Ula.

The children couldn't believe their eyes or their ears. 'Surely cats and dogs don't talk?' the children asked the two animals in front of them.

'We *do* talk,' explained Catvinkle. 'We talk all the time, but humans almost never pay us any attention.'

'It's true,' added Ula. 'No offence, but most humans are so busy worrying about themselves that they hardly ever give a thought to other animals who might be talking to them, often with very interesting things to say.'

'Yes,' agreed Catvinkle, 'but to be fair to the humans, we only ever try to talk to special humans who seem friendly, kind and calm, and who smell nice.'

'You two seem very nice and you smell a bit like Mr Sabatini,' said Ula.

'Hey, that's true!' said Catvinkle, pleasantly surprised at her dog friend's powers of observation. 'What a powerful snout you have, Ulee.' Then, turning to the children, she added, 'It might be because he's just given you each a haircut. His paws would have been all over you.'

The children looked at each other, still completely stunned to find that the lovely cat and dog they had wanted to pat in Mr Sabatini's hair salon earlier were now talking to them and to each other.

'So, at first I thought I heard crying and then very

soon after I thought I heard laughing. Am I right?' asked Ula.

'Yes,' said Anja. 'Ferdi was crying because we've been trying to be so brave while our parents are away for work. We've been staying with our aunt, who is nice, but we've been missing our parents terribly and we hadn't cried at all, neither of us.'

'But then,' continued Ferdi, 'we lost our favourite toy and it was too much for me to bear. It was a toy Mum and Dad gave us and we loved playing with it. They had given it special powers. It was like magic.'

'What was it?' asked Ula.

'It won't sound very special when I tell you about it but it is,' said Ferdi. 'It's just a rubber ball. It's made of clear rubber but it's colourful in the middle where it sort of sparks in flashes that look like bolts of lightning when it bounces or hits anything.'

'It always seemed that it was shooting sparks of our parents' love as we played with it, and it helped us to feel they were with us while they are away for work, but now it's gone,' said Anja.

'Hmmm . . . this is very sad, too sad to bear,

even if we're not any of us actually bears,' said Catvinkle. 'We will help you to find your ball, won't we, Ulee?'

'Yes,' said Ula, 'we will help you.'

'We like helping,' said Catvinkle. 'Especially Ulee. I'm not saying I don't like helping because I do, but Ulee likes helping even more than I do.'

'Do you think so?' asked Ula.

'Oh yes, definitely more than me.'

'Gee, Catvinkle, I had no idea I liked helping more than you do.'

'No point hiding it, Ulee, you're quite the helping kind. I could learn a lot from you when it comes to helping.'

Catvinkle suggested to the children that they not mention any of this to their aunt. 'No offence to your aunt but her hair reminded me of a beehive even before she asked to have it styled like one.'

'Oh yes, I see what you mean,' agreed Ula.

'If she were to give any shelter to bees in her hair it could be very bad for us,' said Catvinkle.

'Oh, I don't think she would ever do that,' said Anja.

'No, not our aunt. She really means well,' added Ferdi.

'Maybe,' said Catvinkle, 'but with hair like that – all tall and honeycomb-like – well, we don't really feel we should trust her with our secrets.'

'Did you say "secrets"?' asked Ula.

'Shh! Never mind our secrets, Ulee. Now, Anja and Ferdi, you've told us what your ball looked like but do you know where you lost it?'

'Can it be lost if they know where it is?' asked Ula.

'Not sure. Good question, Ulee, let's ask them and see,' said Catvinkle.

CHAPTER 9

Ferdi and Anja explained that they did know where their ball was but they were afraid to go and get it.

'Do you believe in ghosts?' asked Ferdi.

'Well, I'm a cat and, as you probably know, we cats have nine lives, so I kind of *have* to believe in ghosts. We're brought up that way from the time we're kittens but I'm perfectly comfortable talking to people and animals who don't believe in ghosts. Why do you ask?'

'Well, we don't really believe in ghosts but we've heard people describe the house where the ball got lost as being the big old ghost house way down the end of Herring Street with the big scary grey dog.

I don't actually know why they call it a ghost house. It's not run-down or anything. The really scary thing about it is the big grey dog. Do you know the house we mean?'

'I know that dog!' said Catvinkle. 'His name is Grayston. I hate that dog! He's so scary I sometimes have to go out of my way to Kittens Anonymous just to avoid him. Some say his bark is worse than his bite, which means his bite must be absolutely terrible because his bark makes my chest all tense and achy. I even practise not thinking about him because I don't want to accidentally think about him when I'm not ready.'

'That might be the big scary dog that chased me when I was trying to get back to the house where I used to live! I sure hope not,' said Ula. She was starting to look a little worried.

'The real reason the house is so scary is because of that dog. Without the dog it would just be a big old house and I quite like a lot of old houses,' said Anja.

'Ferdi and Anja, I have a question, if you don't mind,' said Catvinkle.

'Yes?' said Ferdi.

'Well, we heard you crying and now we know it was over losing the special ball your parents gave you. But then we heard you laughing quite suddenly. What made you laugh like that?'

'We saw what seemed to be you kissing Ula's snout,' said Anja. 'It was very funny!'

'I was going for the salmon!' Catvinkle protested.

'We don't care,' said Ferdi.

'Neither do *I*,' said Ula.

'But Ulee, tell them about the salmon, how I was going for the salmon!'

'Catvinkle was going for the salmon,' said Ula in an attempt to back up her friend.

'Well, it was a beautiful thing to see,' said Anja.

'Of course,' said Catvinkle. 'Salmon is always a beautiful thing.'

'Can you really help us get our special ball back?' asked Ferdi.

Catvinkle promised them that she and Ula would get their special ball back, and the children went back into the salon. Now, though, both children were happy. They were going to get their special ball back from the big scary grey dog, and on top of this, they had enjoyed their first ever conversation with a cat and a dog.

All of this made Catvinkle happy too. Looking into the salon, she saw Mr Sabatini saying goodbye to the aunt and the children.

'Ulee, come and look at the aunt's hair. It is a beehive, all right. It's not Mr Sabatini's fault, I'm sure. She probably asked for something stinging insects would be happy to live in. Some people are like that. You ever met one of those people, Ulee?'

'Catvinkle,' said Ula with slight worry in her voice, 'do you mind if I change the subject for a moment?'

'I was going for the salmon!!!' Catvinkle said.

'No, it's not about that. You know how you promised Anja and Ferdi we'd get their special ball back, the one their parents gave them, from the big scary grey dog, Grayston?'

'Yes?' said Catvinkle.

'How are we going to do that?' asked Ula.

'Well, knowing how much you like helping

people, I knew you'd try really hard to get the children's ball back to make them happy. That's why I was so confident when I offered to help them.'

'What part do you think *you'll* play?' asked Ula.

'Planning, Ulee. I'll be in charge of planning and thinking about the whole thing from start to finish. I won't stop thinking about the whole thing until you've got the ball safely back,' said Catvinkle.

'Catvinkle,' asked Ula, 'why are you doing the planning and thinking and I'm the one going to see the big scary grey dog to get the ball back?'

'It's a good question, Ulee.'

'Thank you. You're too kind,' said Ula.

'Don't mention it. What was the question again?'

'Why are you doing the planning and thinking and I'm the one actually going to get the ball back?' Ula asked again.

'Well, first,' said Catvinkle, 'I already thought of the idea of us making the children happy by getting the ball for them. This means that when it comes to thinking about it, I was way ahead of you. You'd probably never catch up, especially if I don't stop thinking about it, which I won't. I didn't want you to feel like a stupid dog, so I took responsibility for the planning and thinking to spare your feelings. You can thank me later.

'Second, I'm absolutely terrified of Grayston, the big scary grey dog. Just thinking about him makes my fur stand on end, and nobody thinks I look very attractive when my fur stands on end.

'Third, I have to practise my baby-shoe dancing for the competition if I'm to win my title back again. I know you really want me to win, and I don't want to let you down. I've got your interests at heart yet again.

'Fourth – and this is important – you're a dog, no offence. I mean, as much as I like you and admire your musky smell, *you're* a dog and Grayston's a dog. You will talk to him and you will be able to make him see reason, dog to dog. But I'm a cat and he would chase me and bark at me and I don't even want to think about what else he might do.

'So, there you have it. After all that explaining I could really use some musk. Do you mind if I just climb atop your back for a while?' Catvinkle jumped up, flopped down on Ula's back and gently sniffed her fur.

'But Catvinkle,' said Ula, 'I'm scared of Grayston too! Just because I'm a dog doesn't mean he's going to like me or that I'll like him.'

'Really?' asked Catvinkle.

'Yes! Remember, I told you I was chased by a big scary dog? Some dogs are nice and friendly but some are awful and scary. Aren't there cats you don't like?'

'Oh yes, Twinkiepaws, I *really* don't like her. I don't even like looking at her. She thinks she's the best dancer in the whole of Kittendom. I hope she coughs on her own fur balls. I had a dream once where I jumped on her tail.'

'Gee, that's not very nice,' said Ula.

'I know, but I only dreamed it. I didn't actually do it so I'm still a very nice cat with impeccable manners. You can't peck my manners. No one can. They're impeccable. Why can't Twinkiepaws see how lovely I am and quit baby-shoe dancing altogether and let me win first prize in the competition again?' Catvinkle stopped, slightly out of breath. 'Sorry, Ulee, I got a little carried away. I take your point. You're scared of Grayston too. I'll admit, that *is* a problem. You promised the children you'd help them. So . . . what are you going to do?' Catvinkle asked her friend.

'I think I'm going to need the help of my cousin, Lobbus,' said Ula.

'Is Lobbus a Dalmatian too?' asked Catvinkle. 'I only ask because I'm interested in your family. It has nothing to do with musk.'

'No, Lobbus is a Russian wolfhound. He's very clever, and he gives good advice because he's travelled around so much and seen so much of the world. And he has a charming Russian accent. He's also very brave. In fact, you may know of him by his full name, "Lobbus the brave dog Lobbus"?'

'No, I can't say I know him by that name either,' said Catvinkle. 'Clever, gives good advice and with a charming Russian accent, also very brave. You didn't really say anything about musk. Does he, for example, smell musky?'

'It's hard for me to say,' said Ula. 'I can't even smell my own musk.'

'Oh yes, that's right,' said Catvinkle. 'It's one of the great sadnesses of nature.'

CHAPTER 10

The next day, Ula visited her cousin, Lobbus the brave dog Lobbus, who lived in a house by the canal on Prince Street or, as the humans called it, Prinsengracht.

The two dogs were very happy to see each other and barked little barks of happiness and sniffed each other's tails, going round and round in a circle for quite a few minutes. Then, somewhat out of breath, they sat down in front of the house where Lobbus lived and looked out at the passing boats as they floated along the beautiful canal. Lobbus offered Ula some water from his water bowl.

'Ula, my dear cousin, how good it is to see you again. What is your news?'

So Ula told her cousin, Lobbus the brave dog Lobbus, all that had happened from the time she came back from Puppies Anonymous and found her painted house all closed up, about getting chased by the big scary grey dog that was probably Grayston, and then about getting caught in the rain twice and not being able to shake off the wet dog smell that the humans at the front desks of hotels didn't like.

'What are you talking about? You smell great, as good as always,' said Lobbus, reassuringly, before adding, 'And *I* just spent five minutes going round in circles smelling your tail! So I'm very up to date on this matter.'

Ula continued with her story, telling Lobbus how kind Mr Sabatini had been, how she ended up in a room with Catvinkle, who seemed to have become her friend, and how she now found herself preparing to go to the home of a big scary grey dog in order to help Anja and Ferdi get their favourite ball back.

'Wait a minute, you said this new friend, Catvinkle, is a cat, yes?' asked Lobbus.

'Yes, she's a cat,' said Ula.

'Are you sure you can trust her?'

'Well, she seems very nice,' said Ula.

'A cat who seems very nice,' said Lobbus, more to himself than to Ula as they continued to look at the canal. 'Ula, you know me, I've met a lot of animals in my many travels over the years, and I've always found that it's helpful to try to get along with them. I once shared a train carriage with a llama. He had some business in Vladivostok – one of his children wanted a position in their zoo. This llama – Roy Llama was his name, and still is – said to his son, "No, not Vladivostok Zoo until I can check it out for you." I admired his love for his children and told him so. We shared a water bowl and talked for hours into the night. A delightful fellow! At the end we sniffed tails and told each other we'd try to keep in touch. And we have. In fact, I'm due to be meeting Roy Llama tomorrow to play backgammon.'

'Really?' asked Ula.

'Yes, and that's not the most amazing part. This is the same Roy Llama who helped me trace some of our family tree. It turns out – if you go back far enough – we're distantly related to a llama on your mother's side.'

'Wow!' said Ula with excitement.

'So you see I'm open-minded to many animals. But,' said Lobbus with some concern in his voice, 'this Catvinkle is a cat. She volunteered you to help the children, she's not going to be there, and now you have to go to see Grayston all by yourself?'

'But Catvinkle told the children I wanted to help them and it's true. I do like helping.'

'You were always a good dog, loving and trusting, right from the time you were a puppy. But perhaps you've been too trusting this time. I hate to say this and to make you doubt your new friend, but this Catvinkle *is* a cat. And we are dogs.'

'Lobbus, what should I do? Will you help me? Will you come with me to help me get the children's ball?'

Lobbus thought for a moment and then said, 'Oh, Ula, I sniff your tail, I share water and snacks with you, I share great news about our family's connection to llamas, but this magic ball business has me worried. Are you sure it's not a cat trick that could get us both into trouble at the paws of another dog, and then Catvinkle will have her room back all to herself?'

Ula thought about this. It was a horrible thought. After a moment she came to the conclusion that she had to be brave and trust her heart.

'She really is my friend, Lobbus. She's even told me her secrets.'

'Secrets! What secrets?' asked Lobbus.

'She has three secrets.'

'Really, what are they?'

'I can't tell you. She made me promise.'

'My dear Ula, I'm a dog *and* your cousin. You can tell me. Perhaps if I know her secrets I can help you solve this problem that your new kitten friend has so generously given you while she stays home by the fire.'

Ula didn't know what to do. She was bred to chase fire trucks, which didn't require as much thinking in a month as she was having to do this week. She was tired, mainly around her head.

'Okay, I'll tell you the first one of the three secrets but then I'll have to stop.'

'All right, tell me the first one,' said Lobbus.

Ula took a deep breath and said, 'She only has two secrets.'

'I thought you said she has three?' said Lobbus.

'Yes, I did. That's her first secret.'

'What is?' asked Lobbus.

'That she only has two secrets,' answered Ula.

'That's her first secret?' asked Lobbus in disbelief.

'Yes,' answered Ula.

'Gee, I would never have guessed that,' said Lobbus.

'No, of course not, it's a secret. You mustn't tell,' said Ula.

'I promise I won't tell, not even a kind-hearted llama would I tell,' said Lobbus. 'Okay, I've got an idea. If Catvinkle will meet with me and discuss the whole Grayston-rubber-ball matter with me then I will help you. But if she won't meet with me, I say it's too dangerous for both of us.'

CHAPTER 11

Ula went back to Mr Sabatini's house without getting lost, which was one good thing, and without any scary animals chasing her, which was another good thing. She told Catvinkle that her cousin, Lobbus, the brave dog Lobbus, would help them to help the children get their ball back, but only if Catvinkle would meet with him.

But Catvinkle said she would be unable to go and meet Lobbus.

'Why?' asked Ula.

'Well, first, he's a dog and, no offence, I can't be seen talking to dogs because it might get back to the other cats at Kittens Anonymous, and then they would tease me and not talk to me. Second, I need to spend all my spare time practising my baby-shoe dancing.'

'But,' said Ula, 'if Lobbus was seen by other dogs talking to *you*, they might tease him and not talk to him or play with him.'

'Really?' said Catvinkle. 'I had no idea dogs could be so catty!'

'So you see, Lobbus would be taking a risk too,' pleaded Ula.

'Yes,' said Catvinkle, 'but he's brave. The word "brave" is even part of his name, Lobbus the brave dog Lobbus.'

Just then Catvinkle and Ula heard a voice joining their conversation. The voice had a Russian accent and it said, 'Yes, but it's a family name passed down from Lobbus to Lobbus. It's a mistake to take too much from a name. If, for example, my name were "Rose" I would still smell like a Russian wolfhound, which, of course, is good, especially for a Russian wolfhound.'

It was Lobbus himself, who had come all the way

to Mr Sabatini's house and sneaked in through the back door to join the conversation.

'Allow me to introduce myself,' he said. 'I am Lobbus the brave dog Lobbus. You must be Catvinkle.' And with old-world charm he gave a very little sniff in the direction of Catvinkle's tail before briefly offering Catvinkle his tail to sniff.

'I *am* Catvinkle,' she said.

Catvinkle loved her new friend Ula and her musk, but now there were two dogs in her room, which was two more than there had been the day before. What if other cats saw her hanging around with these two dogs? What if there were to be *more* dogs coming? She was currently outnumbered by dogs in her own room. This had never happened before and Catvinkle had been brought up to be frightened by something like this. Was this part of some doggy trick to trap an innocent cat?

'Ulee, why is he here with us?' Catvinkle asked, trying not to sound nervous.

'Lobbus, what made you come here? I thought I was going to ask Catvinkle to come and meet *you*,' asked Ula of her cousin, Lobbus.

'Why am I here?' asked Lobbus the brave dog Lobbus, without expecting either of the other two to answer. 'I'll tell you why I'm here. I knew from the top of my tail to the claws in my paws that Catvinkle wouldn't be brave enough to come out and just talk with me about the plan to get the magic ball for the children. And it's all because

I am a dog. You say I am brave. Well, yes, I'm brave. That's why I came here.' He turned to Catvinkle. 'But what of your friend, my cousin, Ula? She is not famous for being brave.'

'No, I'm famous for always having the smell of a wet dog, even when I'm completely dry,' said Ula.

'My cousin Ula here has a musky smell that you love. All right, you can love it. But what can you do to help her and make her happy in the way that a good friend does? You send her off in the direction of Grayston, a big and scary dog in anyone's language.'

'But I didn't *know* dogs were scared of other dogs when I came up with my plan,' explained Catvinkle.

'All right, so you didn't know. But *now* you know,' said Lobbus, 'and nothing changes. Still your plan has Ula going to get the ball from Grayston all by herself. I'm sorry, Ula,' said Lobbus to Ula, 'this is unfortunately the way of the cat. I was pretty sure this is what your new friend, Catvinkle, would say and that's why I came here without waiting for you to report back.'

'But Ulee,' said Catvinkle, 'you know I have to practise my you-know-what for the you-know-what competition and I did my part already by thinking hard and coming up with the plan to make the children happy.'

'Forgive me, Catvinkle, but your plan is a terrible plan for Ula. She does most of the work and takes all of the risk,' said Lobbus.

'But Ulee, you must admit, you like helping people even more than I do,' implored Catvinkle.

This last remark made Lobbus a bit angry and he raised his voice because he thought his cousin was being tricked.

'You think you can use her niceness against her? Listen, Catvinkle, I once rode on a flatbed truck for eleven days with an ant-eating echidna all the way to the freezing wastelands of Yakutsk. When we got there the ground was frozen so hard that the echidna had no way of digging into the ground and reaching the ants he needed, and he cried all the way back. For eleven days I sat and listened to that echidna! I had to put my front paw on its back to try to comfort it while it cried for lack of ants. Do you know how prickly is the back of an echidna? Do you know how it feels to have your front paw bouncing up and down on the spiky back of an echidna as the truck goes over bump after bump on the road for eleven days?!'

Catvinkle turned to Ula and lifted her front paws up in the air in a shrug. 'I have no idea what your cousin Lobbus is talking about,' said Catvinkle.

'I think he means that he's seen a lot in his life as a well-travelled Russian wolfhound and that he isn't easily tricked. Not that I'm saying you're trying to trick me. But . . . are you trying to trick me, Catvinkle?'

Before she could answer, Lobbus the brave dog Lobbus jumped back into the conversation.

'Catvinkle, don't try to pull the fur over my eyes,' said Lobbus, enjoying the freedom from good manners that comes with interrupting.

'I'm not trying to pull the fur over your eyes, Lobbus. I think it just falls that way naturally, especially when you get cross. And I'm not trying to trick you, Ulee. But Lobbus is right, I am a cat and so I do what cats *naturally* do. I can't help it. Even the best of us might not be quite as helpful as a wonderful dog like you. You see, the help I could give you if I were to come to scary Grayston's house is very small. But if I stay here and practise my you-know-what for the you-know-what competition I'll be giving myself a lot of help – a lot, a lot!' said Catvinkle.

CHAPTER 12

Ula was looking sad. Lobbus decided to take her outside for a long walk to try to comfort her.

They went from the canal on Herring Street, with its beautiful cobblestones and lovely old gable houses all crammed together as though cuddling each other, down to the smaller Lilly Canal.

'I thought she was my friend,' said Ula.

Seeing Ula was not yet feeling better, Lobbus took her even further. They walked to the corner of Prince's Canal and Brewer's Canal, to the famous Cafe Puppy Land, where dogs had been resting, drinking and snacking since 1642. They let people in there as well but humans got the name wrong, as they so often did, calling it Cafe Papeneiland.

Inside Cafe Puppy Land were interesting paintings of old Amsterdam on the wooden walls, showing visitors how Amsterdam used to look. But Lobbus suggested they sit outside on the street to better enjoy looking at the view of boats on the canal and at the beautiful green leaves fluttering on the branches of the elm trees.

An Old English sheepdog came out from the cafe to take their order, but Ula was too mopey to have anything but water.

'I'm not saying she's *not* your friend,' said Lobbus, 'but she's a cat. It's the cats, they can't help themselves. I think they're brought up that way – but don't tell anyone I said that. You, though, Ula, are a wonderful big-hearted dog. Do you still really want to try to help the children?'

'Yes, we *have* to try. We promised them we would.'

'All right then,' said Lobbus, 'I will help you. We will be a team, you and me.'

'And Catvinkle?' asked Ula with hope in her voice.

'Well, she's probably done all the work she's going to do on this plan. Come on, let's talk and work out a new plan on the way to Grayston's home. I know you're probably thinking about your friend Catvinkle. Is she a good friend or a bad friend? Cats can be hard for us to understand. We're dogs – we shouldn't feel bad if we don't understand them. The best thing to do now is to concentrate on getting the magic ball back for the children.'

The two dogs decided to take a boat along the canal from Cafe Puppy Land all the way to Grayston's house. While Ula still felt confused about her cat friend, Catvinkle, it did feel good to spend this time with her cousin, Lobbus.

'What's the first thing to do?' Lobbus asked Ula.

'I don't know,' said Ula.

'The first thing to do is not panic,' said Lobbus.

'What do you mean "panic"?' asked Ula.

'Okay,' said Lobbus, 'you know when you're so frightened that your thoughts go round and round in a circle as though they had tails, and each thought wants to chase the tail of the thought up ahead, but the thoughts never come up with anything except reminders of how scared you are?'

'Yes, I know that feeling very well,' said Ula.

'That's panic, Ula, and we mustn't do it. No good can come from it. Here's what we do to stop that horrible panicky feeling. What I'm about to tell you is a strategy that's been handed down from one Lobbus to another over many generations. Are you ready to learn Lobbus's famous panic-stopping strategy, dear cousin Ula?'

'I think I am,' said Ula.

'Okay, listen carefully. To stop panic we have to think of all the little steps we have to take, one at a time, in order to do whatever it is we're trying to do when we hear the galloping hooves of panic chasing after us. Think of the steps but just *one at a time*. Never more than one at a time. Panic hates it when you're concentrating on something else. So if ever you're starting to panic, always remember your cousin Lobbus saying, "one at a time". Imagine you're walking through a forest and looking at the leaves, not the trees.'

'What do you mean?' asked Ula.

'Imagine yourself walking into a forest. Are you imagining, Ula?'

'Yes,' said Ula, closing her eyes.

'Now maybe you're scared, maybe you feel panic coming on. It's galloping after you. Galumph! Galumph! It's getting louder and closer. What should you do? Don't look at all the trees ahead of you, because if you looked at all the trees ahead of you you'd think, "There are too many trees ahead of me and I'll never get out of here." So you don't do that. You just look at one leaf then another leaf, then another leaf, and you keep doing this, leaf after leaf, until you're out of the forest.'

'That sounds like a good idea,' said Ula. 'One at a time, just think of the leaves, one at a time.'

'That's good, Ula. I think you've got it. But if you *do* feel like panicking when you see the big scary grey dog Grayston,' said Lobbus, 'remember, I'll be with you, and remember, also, I'm your older cousin so I'm the leader. I start first. You can't start panicking until I'm finished, and I might never finish panicking. And if I don't ever finish, you can never start. Never!'

Finally they arrived at the house of Grayston. He was widely known as a big scary grey dog because he *was* a big scary grey dog. It was said his bark was as loud as a lion's roar and could be heard up to five kilometres away from his snout. But this had never really been properly tested because it would have taken someone to make him bark and someone else to stand five kilometres away at exactly the same time. While lots of animals had volunteered to stand five kilometres away, no one could be found to be the one to make him bark. Nevertheless, the power of Grayston's scary bark was widely accepted by all the animals who knew him and by many who didn't.

Ula was very scared and Lobbus the brave dog Lobbus was pretty scared too.

But Lobbus had a plan. Ula would go around the side of the old grey house and see if she could see the ball though a gap in the fence, while Lobbus would try to negotiate with Grayston for the ball to be returned.

Ula sneaked around the side as quietly as an excitable Dalmatian could. She could see a secret garden hidden from the street. It was much larger than anyone looking from outside would have imagined and very beautiful. Surrounding the lush green grass were thickly branched olive trees, tall green spruce trees and several one-hundred-year-old wisteria bushes, some with blue-violet flowers, some with white flowers and some with purple flowers. In the centre of it all was a small pond with very smooth stones at the bottom and a sculpture of a prancing horse at one end.

Wow, thought Ula, so this is where you get to live if you're scary!

Meanwhile, at the front garden, Lobbus was offering some introductory barks in Grayston's direction.

'Excuse me, you are Mr Grayston, the big scary grey dog?' asked Lobbus the brave dog Lobbus, trying to be politely unafraid.

'Some say I'm scary. Who are you?' said Grayston, coming to the fence to talk to Lobbus.

'My name is Lobbus the brave dog Lobbus. I would offer you my tail to sniff but, as you can see, the fence makes this an impossibility. Perhaps you've heard of me.'

'No, never. Why should I have heard of you? I've never heard of you,' said Grayston, unimpressed.

'Really? I'm quite well known in Vladivostok and Yakutsk and in many other places too. I thought a dog of the world such as yourself – a dog with such an obvious interest in current events, like, say, the recent news of a missing rubber ball that came to someone it didn't belong to – might have heard of me.'

'Well, you're wrong. I've never heard of you.'

'Now that you *have* heard of me,' said Lobbus, 'I thought you might enjoy negotiating with me. Do you enjoy negotiating?'

'I don't know what that is. Anyway, what are you doing at my fence? Don't you know my house is possibly haunted and that I'm very, very scary?' asked Grayston.

'Oh yes, I know that, which is why I thought,

"Poor Grayston, he probably never gets to negotiate with anyone and he's missing out on so much fun."'

'What's negotiating, again?' asked Grayston, a little embarrassed that he didn't know what the word meant.

Lobbus sensed that Grayston was embarrassed and so he asked, 'Is "negotiating" one of those words that you used to understand perfectly but, because you're tired and possibly hungry, its meaning now suddenly escapes you, like a ball that has rolled under a fence and has escaped its rightful owners?'

'Yes,' said Grayston, 'it *is* one of those words.'

'Oh, I see,' said Lobbus. 'Allow me to remind you what negotiating is. Here's how negotiating works. You'll love it! We choose something – like a clear rubber ball with colours that sparkle when it's bounced – and we go back and forth in a conversation offering each other things until we both end up with something we want. I might get the rubber ball and you might get something else that *you* want.'

'But I've got everything I want,' said Grayston.

'No, you *don't* have everything you want. I know something you want that you don't have, and I could get it for you.'

'What is it?' asked Grayston, starting to show interest in the negotiation.

'Oh no, not so fast, my scary grey negotiating partner. Before I tell you what you want, I have to see the rubber ball to be sure that it's safe and in good condition.'

'I don't have any rubber ball,' said Grayston.

'Mr Grayston, I do hope you won't be offended if I remind you of something that you already know.'

'What is it?' asked Grayston.

'That you're lying,' said Lobbus.

'How do you know I'm lying?'

'Because witnesses have seen you with the ball in this very garden.'

'This very *what* garden?' asked Grayston.

'Show me that ball and I'll describe your garden for you,' said Lobbus.

'What?' said Grayston. 'You're getting me all confused and it's giving me a headache.' Grayston wasn't used to this much conversation. Usually he had only to run up to the fence looking scary and other dogs would run five kilometres, preferring to try to hear a lion's roar than to see, even for one second, Grayston's gnashing teeth inside his scary snout.

'I can stop your headache,' said Lobbus. 'Just show me that the rubber ball is safe and in good condition and I'll take your headache away.'

'But aren't I still denying that I *have* the rubber ball?' asked Grayston, now quite confused.

'No, that was before your headache. Now you're admitting it,' said Lobbus.

'I don't want to talk to you,' said Grayston.

'It's too late, we're already talking.'

'Are we negotiating?' asked Grayston.

'Yes, yes, as a matter of fact we are, and you're doing a *fabulous* job,' said Lobbus. 'I can see you do this a lot.'

CHAPTER 13

All this time Ula was around the side of the house, having squeezed through a gap in the fence, trying to see inside the secret hidden garden in the hope of finding the ball. She was terrified that she would make a sound that would attract the attention of Grayston, who would come and bark at her and maybe do something even worse.

She couldn't see the ball at all and was feeling scared. She wished she could be of more help to Lobbus, who was bravely talking to Grayston through the front fence all by himself. 'One leaf at a time, one leaf at a time,' she said to herself to keep the panic away while she looked for the ball.

It seemed to be working. What good advice! What a great cousin!

Suddenly, Ula felt a tiny breath of warm wind on her ear. She didn't know what it was, but before she could look up or get too scared she heard a whisper.

'Ulee, it's me!'

It was Catvinkle, hovering in the air with the big red bow on her tail spinning incredibly fast like the propeller on a helicopter.

'Catvinkle, what are *you* doing here?' Ula asked, in a very quiet voice so that Grayston wouldn't hear.

'I was at home in front of the fire practising my baby-shoe dancing for the competition tomorrow, but I found that I couldn't concentrate because I felt bad inside. At first I thought it was the salmon I ate yesterday but then I remembered that you ate it too and that you weren't feeling bad inside.'

'Yes, I was.'

'Do you think it was the salmon?'

'No.'

'No, neither do I,' said Catvinkle. 'What could possibly be bad about salmon – other than that

it's not herring? I realised that I felt bad inside for a number of reasons, none of which have salmon in them.'

'What are they?' asked Ula.

'First, I missed you. I think you've become my best friend. I never expected a dog to be my friend *at all*, let alone my best friend, but here you are. Second, I was ashamed that I wasn't doing more to help you get the ball back for the children. Something your cousin, Lobbus the brave dog Lobbus, said really stuck in my head.'

'What was it?' Ula enquired.

'Lobbus said that I wasn't up to helping more because I am a cat. But I didn't feel right about that. Just because someone says they don't think you can do something doesn't mean you have to agree with them, right? We don't have to be what someone else says we are. I wanted to prove Lobbus wrong. When you left I wondered if a cat really *could* do more to help. I realised that the only way to know for sure was to try to test myself, even if I have to cope somehow with the salty water,' said Catvinkle.

'What salty water?'

'The salty water in my eyes,' replied Catvinkle. 'It just kept coming and coming like never before. I wanted to be with you either at home or trying to win back the children's ball. I thought that if Grayston did anything wrong to you I would never, ever forgive myself – and I normally forgive myself several times a day.'

Catvinkle's tail stopped spinning and she flopped down on Ula's back and started breathing in the scent of her fur.

'You don't mind, do you? Mmmm, that musk is *so* good!' said Catvinkle. 'I realised while you were gone that I was desperate for some of my best friend's high quality musk. So with all of this in mind, I decided to try to fly further than I've ever flown before to find you. Now my tail is tired from keeping my big red bow spinning like a helicopter propeller. So tired! I'm so tired that I forgot the other thing I really wanted to tell you. Now what was it?'

'Gee, I'm not sure, Catvinkle. I find it hard

enough to remember things *I've* forgotten. I'll never remember something *you've* forgotten.'

'Let's see,' said Catvinkle, trying to remember. 'I was flying . . . my tail was getting tired and sore . . . I saw you from way up in the air, started to lower myself down and . . . Oh yeah! I saw the ball. It's in the house with Grayston's puppies. Who knew that a dog as scary as Grayston would have puppies?'

'You found the ball?!' cried Ula. Unfortunately, in her excitement, she forgot to speak quietly, and Grayston heard her loud bark.

Grayston came bounding at them from around the corner. His huge grey paws were going very fast along the muddy ground and froth was coming out of his mouth as though there was a cappuccino machine in his stomach that had exploded.

'Woof! Woof!' Grayston shouted. 'Woof, and I mean that in a terribly angry and unfriendly manner.'

Ula could hear Lobbus calling from around the corner. 'Wait, Mr Grayston, we haven't finished our negotiations. You could play on and win a car!'

'Quick,' Catvinkle whispered to Ula. 'Go inside the house through that doggie door and get the ball. I'll distract Grayston!'

'No, it's too dangerous for you to stay here, Catvinkle. You're a little cat!' cried Ula.

'No, *you* go, Ulee. I can handle Grayston.'

CHAPTER 14

Big scary Grayston was getting closer and closer. Ula ran into the house through the doggy door. Inside, she found three adorable puppies playing with the children's rubber ball.

'Hello, puppies. My name is Ula. Are you Grayston's puppies?'

'Yes,' said one. 'I'm Graham, this is my brother, Gram, and my sister, Grace.'

'Well, you all look like wonderful puppies. You're a credit to your father,' Ula said, then added under her breath, 'May his scariness find a new target in another life.'

'Thank you, Ms Ula,' said Gram.

'What brings you to our home?' asked Grace.

'Well, I have some friends – human children, small persons – who lost their favourite toy. It's a clear rubber ball that lights up when it bounces. It was given to them by their parents, and now that their parents are away for their work the children love the ball even more. It helps them to feel close to their parents. But yesterday they lost it in someone's garden and now they are very sad. They lost it around here and so I'm looking for it.'

The three puppies looked at each other. All at once, at exactly the same time, three little tails stopped wagging.

'Excuse me, Ms Ula, do you mind if we have a quick family meeting?' said Graham.

Before Ula even had a chance to answer, the three young puppies had formed a triangle with their three heads. In the middle of the triangle of heads was the rubber ball. All Ula could see was three little tails sticking up and wagging very quickly in the air around the ball as they whispered to each other.

Finally the three puppies turned back around to face Ula.

'Ms Ula,' said Gram, 'we think *this* ball might be the children's ball.' He pushed the ball towards Ula with his snout.

'And,' said Grace, 'we would like the children to have it back if it means so much to them.'

'That's so kind of you, puppies. What good dogs you are!'

'There's just one thing we would ask in return,

Ms Ula,' said young Graham. 'Please could you tell us the secret?'

'The secret! How did you know about the secret?' said Ula. 'I don't think I *can* tell you, even though you're such lovely puppies.'

'Please tell us the secret of how you get human children to play with you and be your friends,' said Grace.

'Oh!' said Ula. 'That's no secret at all. You just have to be nice and friendly to them. You mustn't be scary. Not like, well, some dogs, who can be a bit scary . . . even to dogs. But the ones with human friends, well, you'll find that they're not scary at all. They're nice and friendly.'

At that very moment, outside in the garden, Grayston was barking wildly at Catvinkle.

Catvinkle had flown up in the air and landed on a branch of a nearby tree. Grayston was jumping up and down on his two back paws trying to reach her, but she was too high.

Lobbus had rushed around from the front to the side fence to help. Using his tail, he beckoned Ula to bring the ball and escape while Grayston was barking fiercely at Catvinkle.

'Thank you for returning the ball, puppies,' Ula said. 'But now I have to run!'

She picked up the ball in her mouth and leapt back through the doggy door.

Grayston spotted Lobbus and Ula trying to run away and he chased after them. He was getting closer and closer to them when he felt a nip on his nose.

'Owww!!! What was that?' shouted the panting, frothing at the mouth Grayston.

It was Catvinkle. She had swooped down from the branch and given Grayston the most unexpected nip on his snout he had ever got in years of fights with many big and scary dogs.

'How dare you! You're a rotten little cat!' Grayston shouted as Lobbus and Ula, now out of the garden, ran away along the street in the direction of Anja's and Ferdi's house.

'How *dare* I?' asked Catvinkle. 'You really want to know? I dare like . . . *this*!'

She flew down again right into the face of the angry Grayston and gave him another nip. These tiny nips were not sharp enough to hurt his snout – but his pride as a big scary dog was in tatters all around him.

'And I'm not a *rotten* little cat,' called Catvinkle. 'I'm an *excellent* little cat!'

With that, she flew over Grayston's fence and

caught up to Lobbus and Ula, who had just arrived at the home of Anja and Ferdi. The three of them were out of breath but extremely happy at their big day's work.

The children were very happy to see them – and that was even before they had realised that their ball was being returned.

'Thank you so very much for getting us our ball back,' said Anja, delighted to see it again.

'You are all so brave,' said Ferdi as the three animals took their share of pats, cuddles and kisses.

Ula introduced her cousin, Lobbus the brave dog Lobbus, to the children. He turned to offer them his tail to sniff, forgetting for a moment that humans don't do that. Then he asked the children a question.

'Can I ask you, Anja and Ferdi, what makes you say this rubber ball is magic? What power does it have?'

'Well,' said Ferdi, 'right from the time our parents gave it to us we would play with it all over the house, in the hallway, in the garden and even on the street sometimes. At the end of every day we always thought we'd lost it. We just couldn't find it and had to stop looking because it was time for bed.'

'Yes,' continued Anja, 'but then every morning when we woke up, the ball was there back in our room on the bookshelf between our beds. It was magic! The ball got itself back to where it wanted to be, which was just where *we* wanted it to be. Magic!'

The three animals looked at each other and smiled, but the children didn't understand why.

'Why are you smiling?' asked Anja. 'It's true!'

'We believe you,' said Catvinkle. 'It was your parents every day putting back the ball they knew you liked to play with so much.'

'So it's *not* magic?' asked Ferdi.

'Well, it *is* a kind of magic,' said Ula. 'It's a special kind of magic that parents have saved up for their children.'

'Yes,' said Catvinkle. 'It's called "love".'

'And guess what!' said Ferdi. 'We got a letter from our parents and they said they're coming home next week.'

The children were very excited. 'When they come home they're going to take us to the zoo, where there's going to be a new koala visiting!' Anja added.

'I think I know the family of this koala,' said Lobbus. 'I once shared a horse and cart ride with his uncle all the way to Smolensk. A charming koala, he taught me a lot about gum leaves and –'

Catvinkle and Ula were trying not to laugh.

'What is it?' asked Lobbus. 'Why do you laugh? You shouldn't laugh at a koala who's not here to defend himself. It's not good manners.'

Ula whispered to Catvinkle that Catvinkle should be at home practising her baby-shoe dancing for the competition the very next day. The three of them said they looked forward to seeing the children again soon, and then they started on their way back home.

When they reached Lobbus's house, he said that he thought he owed Catvinkle an apology.

'You are a credit to all cats, Catvinkle. I misjudged you and for this I am sorry. You are brave and not entirely lazy. I am proud to call you my friend.'

'Thank you, Lobbus, and I am proud to call you my friend's cousin.'

At this they sniffed each other's tails and then Catvinkle turned to Ula and said, 'Let's go home, Ulee.'

'Okay, Catvinkle, let's go home,' said Ula.

PART THREE

THE COMPETITION

CHAPTER 15

When Ula woke up the next morning, Catvinkle was seemingly asleep, except for one thing: her tail was moving from side to side like windscreen wipers on a car on a rainy day. Curling, uncurling, side to side. Curling, uncurling, side to side. It was fascinating to watch.

'Are you awake?' whispered Ula.

'Only a bit,' said Catvinkle with her eyes closed.

'How can you be a *bit* awake?' asked Ula.

'Well, it takes years of practice, Ulee,' Catvinkle said. 'First, if you wake up and think that you're too sleepy and warm and snuggy to get up out of your basket, you're probably still asleep. My paws are all heavy at such a time. My nose just wants to nuzzle deeper and deeper into my basket. The trick is to try to stop thinking. Who can think while they're asleep? Not this kitten.'

Catvinkle opened one eye. 'Oh no, I'm thinking again. I hope I don't start counting how many days there are until it's my birthday. That would really wake me up. See, Ulee, that's all there is to it. Here I am, warm and snuggy *and* thinking. I must be asleep, but a *bit* awake. I could be fully awake by lunchtime if I really put my mind to it.'

She opened her other eye. 'You should try it sometime, Ulee. You too can be a bit awake if you work at it. Although, you know, if I keep doing all this thinking, my brain is going to wake up and want breakfast.' Catvinkle yawned. 'Hmm ... Breakfast! *Now* I'm awake. Did you say something about my birthday, Ulee? Or was that me?'

Ula tilted her head to the side. 'Catvinkle, don't you think you should be up and practising your baby-shoe dancing? After all, the National Kitten Baby-Shoe Dancing Competition is today.'

'Don't worry, my dear Ulee, I've already started.'

'What have you started?' asked Ula.

'Baby-shoe dancing.'

'But you're still lying in your basket all warm and snuggy,' said the puzzled Ula.

'Yes, but in my basket, underneath my tummy, my paws are going crazy.'

'Really?'

'Oh yes, they're limbering up, moving from side to side. I'm really pleased with all the work they're doing.'

'When will you do the actual dancing? I mean, the part where you're standing up?' asked Ula.

'Soon,' said Catvinkle, stifling another yawn.

'But the National Kitten Baby-Shoe Dancing Competition is later today. There's no time to lose.'

'Oh, Ulee,' said Catvinkle, standing up and stretching first her front paws and then her back paws. 'Time goes on and on and on. So, actually, there *is* time to lose. No one can capture it so it's not really worth talking about. But if you are looking for something to talk about, did you know that my birthday is coming up soon, probably sooner than you realise?'

'I think I need a lick or two of water,' said Ula after that explanation. 'My head hurts a bit from thinking about what you were saying.'

'You must be awake,' said Catvinkle. 'Be careful, Ulee. Thinking's not for everyone. Help yourself to some water. I would like you to think of my water bowl as your water bowl, and don't worry if you can never forget that it was my water bowl first. It is only natural for a lovely and considerate musky dog such as yourself to remember that.'

As she lapped water from the bowl, Ula watched in amazement as Catvinkle stood on her hind legs with her tail in the air, her front paws raised and bent at the elbow. She put one bottom paw in the right baby shoe and one bottom paw in the left.

With her eyes closed, Catvinkle counted softly to herself, 'One, two, three,' and began to dance. She swung her rump to the left and then to the right and back again with her tail going in the opposite direction.

Then in a strange voice she called out what sounded to Ula like very funny words.

'Ah–huh, ching ching, Ah–huh,
   Ah–huh, ting ting, Ah–huh.
Ah–huh, ching ching, Ah–huh,
   Ah–huh, ting ting, Ah–huh.
I'm a winking cat, name of Catvinkle.
I'm a winking cat, name of Catvinkle.
Ah–huh, ching ching, Ah–huh,
   Ah–huh, ting ting, Ah–huh.
Ah–huh, ching ching, Ah–huh,
   Ah–huh, ting ting, Ah–huh.
I wiggle from the middle,
   it's a riddle how I twiddle.
Ah–huh, ching ching, Ah–huh,
   Ah–huh, ting ting, Ah–huh.
Ah–huh, ching ching, Ah–huh,
   Ah–huh, ting ting, Ah–huh.
I'm a winking cat, name of Catvinkle.

I'm a winking cat, name of Catvinkle.
Ah-huh, ching ching, Ah-huh,
    Ah-huh, ting ting, Ah-huh.
Ah-huh, ching ching, Ah-huh,
    Ah-huh, ting ting, Ah-huh.'

Then she got so excited, so caught up in the fun of her baby-shoe dancing, that she jumped up in the air and, because the big red bow on her tail started to spin like the propeller on a helicopter, she hovered in the air and fluttered her thick white whiskers.

'Wow, you're flying again!' cried Ula with amazement.

'Did you like my song? I made it up myself,' Catvinkle asked, getting more and more out of breath. 'Uh-oh, I think I'm going to fall.'

'Would it be okay if you didn't fall on *me*?' Ula asked quickly.

Catvinkle tried to float to the left, away from Ula. By doing so, she hit the ground hard when she fell. *Thump!*

'Oh, the floor is very hard. It was a big mistake not to fall onto your back,' said Catvinkle.

'I'm very sorry for my part in it,' said Ula.

'Never mind, Ulee. Try to forgive yourself even though yours was probably the largest part in the whole incident, up there with gravity. I really need some musky goodness now. Would you mind if I climbed atop your back for a sniff or two?'

Catvinkle hopped up onto Ula's back and buried her face into her friend's fur before Ula even had a chance to reply.

'Oh, that musk! It never fails me! Thanks, Ulee.'

CHAPTER 16

That same morning, in the big old ghost house way down the end of Herring Street, Grayston, a big grey dog said by many to be quite scary, was talking to his three puppy children, Graham, Gram and Grace.

'Why the long faces, my dear puppies? You know that's for horses. We're dogs and proud of it.'

'Yes, Dad,' said Gram rather glumly.

'You don't sound very proud,' said Grayston.

'Why should we be proud, again? Can you remind us, Dad?' asked Grace.

'I'm surprised you ask, my lovely Grace. We should be proud because we're dogs,' answered her father.

'But all we did was get born as dogs. We had no choice in the matter and didn't do anything special. Shouldn't you do something to *earn* the pride – be *good* puppies or do something good?'

'Children, we're dogs! That's a terrific thing to be. Isn't it enough for you to be a dog for you to feel pride?'

'But, Dad,' said Graham, 'some dogs are better than others, right?'

'Oh yes, definitely,' said Grayston. 'Some dogs are much better than others.'

'So some dogs can be bad?' Graham continued.

'Well, I suppose so,' said Grayston, thinking. 'But they're still dogs, which is better than anything else.'

'Why?' asked Grace.

'What? What do you mean "why"?' asked Grayston, who could not believe what he was hearing.

'Why is it better to be a bad dog than a good . . . cat, for instance?'

'We're dogs!' cried Grayston. 'Don't you like being a dog?'

'Yes,' said Grace, 'but why are all dogs, even naughty ones, better than other animals?'

'Grace, my darling puppy,' said Grayston, 'you haven't been the same since that rubber ball was stolen from our family. I know it was a lovely ball that sparkled in the middle when it bounced. It was a rotten cat who took your ball away. Are you feeling unwell?'

'Dad,' said Gram, 'it wasn't our ball.'

'What do you mean? I got that ball for you to play with and you were playing with it in our garden. Of course it was our ball.'

'No, Dad,' said Graham. 'It belonged to some human children. It was a special present from their parents, who had to go away for a while, and the children were playing with it to have fun and to remind them of their parents.'

'Who's been filling your heads with this non-sense? Was it that naughty cat who took your ball?'

'Dad, it wasn't actually a cat who took it. The ball was taken away by a couple of dogs. It was dogs who took it for the children,' said Grace.

'Yes,' said Gram. 'Dogs . . . just like us.'

'What's going on here? My children, you're

making me dizzy! I think I need to get a drink of water. Didn't you like the ball I got you?'

'Yes, Dad,' said Grace. 'We liked it very much, but then we learned it wasn't ours and we felt ashamed.'

'Ashamed!' cried Grayston. 'Ashamed of what?'

'Dad, the ball didn't belong to us. It belonged to two children called Anja and Ferdi.'

'Well, if it belonged to Anja and Ferdi, why didn't they come to collect it?' said Grayston.

'Because they were too scared,' said Gram. 'They were scared of the house but mostly they were scared of . . . you.'

Grayston's paws became a little shaky beneath him and he collapsed to the ground. He hated to think he had caused any unhappiness to his children. Could it be true?

After a moment, he picked himself up, paw by paw, but there were still crinkly creases in his forehead fur just above his eyes.

'Well . . . yes, I am a big scary dog. I thought you liked that. Aren't I the scariest dog in all of Herring Street, maybe even in all of Amsterdam?'

'Yes, Dad, that's why no human children ever come to play with us,' said Graham.

'You *want* human children to come and play with you?' asked Grayston.

'Yes! Dad, there are puppies all over Amsterdam who have lots of human children to play with. They visit each other, they play ball, they play chasey, they bring snacks, they pat the puppies and sometimes they even cuddle the puppies.'

'And this is what you want?' asked Grayston.

'Who wouldn't want lots of human children to be your friends? Only none of them will ever come and play with us,' said Gram.

'No,' said Grace, 'they're too scared.'

Grayston stood perfectly still for a moment, thinking about what his children were telling him.

'Oh my goodness,' said Grayston. 'I've spent my whole life being scary. I've worked hard at it – not just being scary but getting the message out to everyone who passed our house. "Beware of scary dog!" Now everything seems all upside down to me.'

He turned to his children and gave them each a lick on the forehead. 'I love my children more than I can say. I love you more than I even understand. I wake up in the morning and I just love you all up. So what am I to do? I'm an old dog and my children want me to learn some new tricks.'

Graham, Gram and Grace snuggled in close to their father and wagged their tails. They knew that he loved them but hadn't known the love was strong enough to make him try to do at least *some* things differently. What a great dad! They crowded in close together and all three of them buried their snouts into the fur on his chest at the same time. Grayston felt happier now than he ever did scaring people and animals away from the house.

CHAPTER 17

Now that she was fully awake, Catvinkle was nervous. So nervous, in fact, that she wouldn't touch her salmon. She was walking from one end of her room to the other, and when she got to the end of the room she would turn back and go the other way.

'Are you going to finish your salmon or . . .?' asked Ula.

'Or what?' asked Catvinkle innocently.

'Or will it be left to go to waste?'

'I think it's going to be left to go to waste,' said Catvinkle.

Ula thought for a moment before speaking. 'How do you feel about that?'

'I'm fine with it. I'm too nervous about the National Kitten Baby-Shoe Dancing Competition to be at all hungry.'

'Do you think *I* should eat it?' asked Ula.

'Look, you can try. Although, since I'm extremely nervous and since you love me so much, you're probably extremely nervous too. But maybe watching you eat it will make me hungry.'

With that encouragement and having already eaten the salmon that Mr Sabatini had put in a bowl for her, Ula put her snout into Catvinkle's food bowl and started to snack on Catvinkle's salmon.

Catvinkle's tail curled and uncurled, curled and uncurled, as she watched her hungry friend.

'Ulee, you're a genius! It's working! Just watching you eat *my* salmon from *my* bowl is making me hungry.'

But by the time she'd finished saying this, the bowl was empty. Ula had eaten all of Catvinkle's salmon.

A silence hung in the air. They just looked at each other for a moment. Ula tilted her head to the left and then to the right and then back to the middle again. Then Ula spoke.

'Catvinkle, you wouldn't have a very woolly blanket that I could wear, do you?'

'No, why?' asked Catvinkle.

'I'm feeling a little sheepish,' said Ula. 'I'm sorry, Catvinkle, now you're feeling hungry but all your salmon is gone.'

'Never mind,' said Catvinkle. 'I probably shouldn't eat before the baby-shoe dancing competition anyway. Besides, the hunger's gone. I'm starting to get nervous all over again.'

'But you're such a good baby-shoe dancer and you've won the competition before. Why are you so nervous?'

'Because I lost last year to that evil little fur ball, Twinkiepaws. I'm not sure if I told you this but I hate, hate, hate her.'

'No, you told me that you hate her but not that you hate, hate, hate her.'

'Well, I know you better now. There's no point holding anything back. Do you mind if I climb atop you and sniff your musk for a while?'

'Be my guest.'

So Catvinkle climbed on top of Ula and started taking deep breaths with her nose buried into Ula's fur. Within a very short time it seemed to be doing the trick.

'Oh, that's good! That's *so* good! Ulee, that musk is the most beautiful calming smell I've ever smelled. If I could feel this calm at the National Kitten Baby-Shoe Dancing Competition I know I could win.'

This gave Ula an idea. 'Hey, Catvinkle, what if I came with you to the competition? Then just before it was your turn to dance you could take in some of my musk and feel calm enough to win.'

'But Ulee, you can't come. The competition is being held in Vondelpark at Kittens Anonymous. I can't bring a dog to Kittens Anonymous.'

'No, I suppose not.'

'*Definitely* not. You know how those cats feel about dogs.'

'Is it fear, mistrust and dislike?' Ula asked.

'Yes, that's it.'

'But *you* don't think of me that way, do you, Catvinkle? And *you're* a cat!'

'Yeah, but I don't really think of you as a dog. I think of you as my best friend, Ulee.'

'But I'm also a dog.'

'I know, I know. That's why I can't take you to the competition even though your musk would make me all calm inside.'

They both sighed.

'Sigh,' said Catvinkle.

'You can say that again,' said Ula.

'I *can*,' said Catvinkle, 'but do you mind if I *don't*? After all, you've already sighed once yourself.'

'Hey, I've just had an idea!' Ula said. 'I'd better say it out loud before I lose it.'

'Is it a good idea?' asked Catvinkle.

'Mmmm . . . Not sure.'

'Well, say it just in case.'

'What if I came with you to the National Kitten Baby-Shoe Dancing Competition and we told all the cats there that I was a cat?'

Catvinkle didn't seem too excited by this idea. 'No offence, Ulee – and you know this is coming from a place of love – but you look really quite a lot like a dog. A very pretty Dalmatian but, you know, still a dog.'

They both slumped down onto the ground in disappointment.

'*I* know!' said Ula, full of enthusiasm. 'What if we told them I was a cat *dressed* as a dog in a dog disguise because I was a really, really famous cat and didn't want any people or animals to know who I was?'

'Do you think it would work?'

'With every hair on my rump I'm not sure it's a good idea, but at least it's an idea,' said Ula.

'Every hair on your rump!' said Catvinkle. 'That's a lot of musky-smelling hair! That's good enough for me. Let's give it a try!'

'Great!' said Ula, very pleased to have come up with an idea that might help Catvinkle.

'Now,' said Catvinkle, 'we need to think of a cat who's so famous everyone would believe that she chose to disguise herself as a dog. Who's a famous cat around here?'

'You're asking the wrong animal. We dogs don't know that much about cats, even the famous ones,' said Ula.

'Okay, I'll just have to figure *everything* out for myself. Let me see, who's a famous cat? Who?'

'Are you talking to yourself?' asked Ula.

'Yes, sorry if I didn't make that clear enough, Ulee. Although I can understand that you might have thought it was my tummy rumbling. I haven't eaten anything all day.'

'Oh, I know,' said Ula sympathetically.

'Yes, that's right, you do know. Don't keep thinking about it, Ulee. You'll only make yourself upset.'

It was at that moment that Ula's eye fell on a pile of newspapers that Mr Sabatini kept piled up in Catvinkle's room before he sent them to be recycled.

'Are there any famous kittens in the newspaper?' Ula asked.

'Not in the human newspapers, but maybe in the *New Paw Times*,' answered Catvinkle. 'Hey, as a matter of fact, I read an article that said Ketzington was planning a visit to Amsterdam.'

New Paw 🐾🐾 *Times*

KETZINGTON D. KITTEN: SINGING STAR TO VISIT AMSTERDAM

'Who?' asked Ula.

'Ketzington.'

'Who's Ketzington?' Ula asked again.

'Are you serious?' said Catvinkle in amazement. 'You've never heard of Ketzington D. Kitten and the Snufflecats from New York?'

'No, sorry, I haven't,' answered Ula.

'Really? Ketzington is only the biggest singing sensation in all of Kittendom! I thought even dogs would have heard of her.'

'Maybe my cousin, Lobbus the brave dog Lobbus, has heard of her.'

Catvinkle thought for a moment. 'You must know some of her songs without realising that they're hers. Do you know "Stairway to Ketzington"?'

'No.'

'"I've Got My Paw On a String"?'

'No.'

'"Stormy Kitten"?'

'No.'

'"You and the Night and the Kitten"?'

'No.'

'"I've Got You Under My Fur"? "Fascinating Kitten"? "The Lady Is a Cat"?'

'Sorry, no,' said Ula.

'You've never heard of Ketzington? Wow! They even wrote a Broadway musical about her life.'

'What was it called?'

'"Ketz".'

'Never heard of it.'

'She has a deli named after her on the Lower East Side – Ketz's Deli – and they even named one of the famous East Side avenues after her. Surely you've heard of Ketzington Avenue?'

'Sorry, Catvinkle. I'm a dog.'

'I know,' said Catvinkle, 'but . . . you *must* know "I Only Have Paws For You"?'

'I might know that one,' said Ula hopefully.

Catvinkle looked at her carefully to see if she was telling the truth. 'Do you really think you might know that one, or are you just saying that because you want it to be true?'

'Um . . . Could you repeat the question?'

'Would you like me not to?' asked Catvinkle.

'Well, we *could* let the moment pass,' said Ula.

'The point is, Ulee, among cats and kittens everywhere, Ketzington is a hugely famous cat. *And* she's known to be touring Amsterdam this week.'

'So I could come with you to the National Kitten Baby-Shoe Dancing Competition,' said Ula excitedly, '*pretending* to be Ketzington disguised as a Dalmatian dog so that no one will bother her and ask her for a paw print.'

'Yes!' said Catvinkle, full of hope. 'It's such a brilliant idea I can't believe I thought of it.'

'Did I help?' asked Ula.

'I can't believe I thought of it with some help from you,' said Catvinkle, 'and on an empty stomach.'

'Then,' said Ula, 'if you're feeling at all nervous before your baby-shoe dance you can just sniff my fur for musky goodness and you'll feel happy and calm again.'

'Yes,' said Catvinkle. 'And if I'm happy and calm I'll definitely be able to beat that evil little cat, Twinkiepaws.'

'Whom you hate, hate, hate!'

'You have such a good memory for details,' said Catvinkle as she tied her baby shoes around her neck.

CHAPTER 18

'I'm feeling good about this,' Catvinkle said, prancing along the street just slightly ahead of Ula. 'Let's go, Ketzington!'

'Who's Ketzington, again?' Ula called.

Mr Sabatini heard Ula asking this as he watched his two pets leaving the house together to go out for a walk. He heard it as just sounds, not words, but still, it made him very happy to see that they had become such good friends.

Catvinkle was now feeling quite confident about her chances of winning the National Kitten Baby-Shoe Dancing Competition. She told Ula why as they walked the streets of Amsterdam on their way to the Vondelpark.

'First,' she said, 'I have you here with me for that musky smell that I've grown so fond of. Second, as you know, I'm really a very good baby-shoe dancer. Third, it's *my* story so I have to win.'

'What do you mean?' asked Ula, trotting alongside her.

'Well, you know, whenever you read a book, hear a story, see a movie or watch a TV show, the person or animal whose story it is always wins any competition that they're in. And it's *my* story.'

'What do you mean it's *your* story?' asked Ula.

'Well, I'm in it all the time. I'm always with me. Yesterday when I woke up, I was there. This morning too. When I went to Grayston's house to help you get the ball, well, I was there. I'm always there so it must be *my* story.'

'But Catvinkle, what about me?'

'What *about* you, Ulee?'

'I'm here too. In fact, I was with you each time that you've just remembered.'

'Of course you were, my dear Ulee. You're my best friend so you have to be in my story. It's only natural.'

'But maybe it's *my* story.'

'Pardon me?' said Catvinkle.

'Maybe it's *my* story and you're in it too because you're *my* best friend.'

'Oh, I don't think so, Ulee. Before I'd even met you, way back then, you were never in my story, but I was. I've been with me since I was a kitten. So you see, it *has* to be my story. That's one of the reasons why I'll win the National Kitten Baby-Shoe Dancing Competition,' Catvinkle said happily.

Ula wished that she could be as confident as her friend Catvinkle. Although she wasn't going to be dancing in the competition, with every step they took – and they had eight paws between them – she was getting closer to being surrounded by a whole *clowder* of cats who didn't like dogs. She was going to have to pretend to be one of them by not speaking.

'Catvinkle, how will all the cats and kittens at

Kittens Anonymous know I'm Ketzington disguised as a Dalmatian dog?'

'I'll tell them, Ulee.'

'Hmmm . . . I wish I'd checked our plan with my cousin, Lobbus the brave dog Lobbus. Lobbus would know if it's a good plan.'

CHAPTER 19

Not too far away, Lobbus was about to leave home to meet an old friend – a llama named Roy – for a game of backgammon. Suddenly, at the end of his street he saw a big scary grey dog running as fast as it could straight for him. He realised it was Grayston running towards him as fast as Grayston could run – which was very fast indeed.

Oh no, Lobbus thought, Grayston is angry that we took the rubber ball back from him for the children, and now he's after me!

Lobbus started running away from Grayston down the other end of the street. But Grayston was a very fast runner and he was catching up, getting closer and closer.

Grayston was puffing and panting but he managed to call out. 'Lobbus! Hey, Lobbus!'

Lobbus too was puffing and panting, but he turned his head in the direction of Grayston as he was running away from him and said, 'It's not me. You've made a mistake.'

'It *is* you,' called Grayston.

'No, it's someone else entirely, someone who just *looks* like me,' called Lobbus, puffing very hard.

To make matters worse, when he got to King's Square Street, some of the humans from Friend's Herring Shop accidentally got in the way. They were putting up signs, posters and banners telling everyone that tomorrow was the opening of herring season, a day to be celebrated by all. But Lobbus was not so happy to see all of these signs. They forced him to slow down, and now there was nothing between him and Grayston but a table and two chairs.

'Stop running away, Lobbus!' shouted Grayston between puffs.

'I tell you, I'm not running away!' said Lobbus, moving around one side of the table.

'Yes you are!' puffed Grayston as he got to the other side.

'Oh yes, you're right. What I meant to say is, "I tell you, I'm not Lobbus".'

'You're not Lobbus?' asked Grayston, still chasing Lobbus.

'No.'

'But you *are* running away,' said Grayston. He circled around the table trying to catch up with Lobbus, who was also circling around the table as he tried to keep away from Grayston.

'All right, I'll grant you that I am slightly running away, yes, it's true.'

'You sure look like Lobbus,' said Grayston, trying to catch him around the table.

'A lot of people say that,' said Lobbus, trying to pick up speed.

A number of humans who had been standing in line at Friend's Herring Shop waiting to buy some fried cod with chopped onions moved away quickly at the sight of what looked like two crazy dogs running around a table outside.

Then these people narrowly avoided being hit by other people who were riding their bicycles. The bicycle bells suddenly rang out and the people who were almost hit called out 'Sorry!' They didn't know which way to turn.

'If you're not Lobbus, why are you slightly running away?' asked Grayston.

'Because,' puffed Lobbus, 'you *think* I'm Lobbus and I wouldn't want to be Lobbus right now.'

'Why not?' asked a huffing Grayston as he went around the table after Lobbus.

'Because I think you might want to bite Lobbus on the rump,' cried Lobbus.

'No, I don't!' said the puffing Grayston.

'Well, Lobbus doesn't believe you,' said Lobbus, very much out of breath now.

'I thought you said you weren't Lobbus.'

'I'm not. I meant to say, if Lobbus were here he wouldn't believe you.'

'How do you know?' asked Grayston, going

around the table in the direction of Lobbus's tail.

'I know just how Lobbus would react in this situation,' said Lobbus, running around the table.

'How would he react?' asked Grayston.

'He would react very much like me,' said Lobbus.

'Amazing!' said Grayston, still going around the table. 'You and Lobbus don't just *look* alike, you even *think* alike.'

Some of the tourists standing near Friend's

Herring Shop came closer to the table and started taking photos.

'Would you like me to give him a message?' asked the exhausted Lobbus.

'Who?' asked Grayston.

'Lobbus!' said Lobbus as he went around the table.

'Are you sure it wouldn't be too much trouble?' asked Grayston as he went around the table still after Lobbus.

'No, not at all,' said Lobbus, wondering how many times he was going to have to go around the table.

'Okay,' said Grayston, 'please tell Lobbus . . . Oh, I haven't planned out my message properly. I don't want to get it wrong,' said Grayston, still chasing Lobbus.

'Well, do you want to go home, think about it and come back?' asked Lobbus, puffing.

'Will you still be here running around this table when I get back?' asked Grayston.

'I can't see why not,' said Lobbus as he went around the table one more time.

But just then both dogs heard a voice.

'Hey, Lobbus, there you are! I thought we were meant to be playing backgammon.'

Both Lobbus and Grayston stopped to see Roy Llama approaching them in front of Friend's Herring Shop. They each stood on the spot, panting heavily.

Grayston looked hard at Lobbus on the other side of the table. He tilted his head from side to side. Then he started to laugh and laugh.

Lobbus didn't know what was going to happen next. He tried to remember that 'brave' was part of his name as he fought back the feeling of being frightened.

'Ha!' said Grayston. 'That stupid llama thinks you're Lobbus!'

CHAPTER 20

By now, Catvinkle and Ula had almost reached Vondelpark, where the cats and kittens of Amsterdam would meet to let their fur down as part of a club called Kittens Anonymous. This was where the National Kitten Baby-Shoe Dancing Competition was to take place. It wouldn't be long before they were inside Vondelpark. Ula noticed that the closer they got to Vondelpark the more nervous Catvinkle was becoming.

They were walking beside the canal trying not to get in the way of the bicycles the humans were always riding. It wasn't easy. Some of the humans weren't very good riders and some of them were good riders but weren't paying enough attention to the cats and dogs in the street. Typical, thought Catvinkle, always focused on themselves, these humans.

She remembered that Mr Sabatini wasn't like that and she wished he was with them now. If he was standing near her, the humans on their bikes would find it easy to see him and would ride around them. Maybe it was hard for fast-moving humans on their bikes to see a little cat and a dog, Catvinkle thought to herself.

But Mr Sabatini was back at the salon making people's hair look nice. And the waves of humans on their bikes swirling around them on the bumpy cobblestone streets weren't helping Catvinkle's nerves one bit.

'Let's stop and rest for a moment, Catvinkle,' said Ula. 'Hey, look up there! They're so pretty, aren't they?'

Ula used her nose to point upwards to three rose-ringed parakeets, each with bright green feathers, pink stripes around their necks, and red beaks.

They were having a rest in the branches of the elm trees on their way back to Vondelpark, which was, of course, just where Catvinkle and Ula were headed.

Catvinkle agreed they were pretty but, being a cat, it was hard for her not to think of them as food. So unless Ula wanted Catvinkle to climb up the tree to try to catch one or more of the rose-ringed parakeets, it was perhaps not the best distraction for a cat.

'I really shouldn't eat so close to the baby-shoe dancing competition,' said Catvinkle, looking away quite quickly.

Luckily there was another distraction. Everyone, including the humans on their bikes, turned to look at the bicycle fisherman who was coming along the canal in his boat. Wearing an orange suit from top to toe, he was fishing from his boat with the help of a mechanical arm. The arm skimmed the bottom of the canal whenever he pulled a special lever at the bow of the boat. But he wasn't trying to catch fish. He wasn't trying to catch any seafood at all. He was trying to catch bikes. Every time he put the boat's mechanical arm in the water, it came up from the bottom a bit sludgy and holding one, two, three or even four bicycles that had somehow come to rest on the bottom of the canal.

'I've never understood why the humans let their bicycles get so wet,' said Ula, still trying to calm Catvinkle's nerves with distractions. 'Rain is one thing. I know the humans sometimes ride their bikes in the rain – and I'm not one to talk about wet fur. But surely this is going too far. Maybe they're trying to teach the bikes to swim? Can't they see that will never work? I'm no expert, but I blame the wheels.'

Ula turned to Catvinkle but she was still looking nervous, so she went on. 'Oh well, whatever they're thinking, it sure is a beautiful day for bicycle fishing, don't you think?'

But now they had reached the part of Vondelpark the cats called Kittens Anonymous, and there was no distracting Catvinkle from the trouble ahead.

'I probably should have mentioned this earlier,' said Catvinkle, 'but since *you're* the one pretending to be Ketzington, who's a cat, you should probably be quite nervous too.'

'I hadn't thought of that,' said Ula, 'but it makes perfect sense. In fact, just your saying it has helped me to feel nervous quite quickly.'

'Yes, I think it's appropriate,' said Catvinkle to her new best friend.

Ula noticed that there were cats and kittens all around them, heading to the same place. Suddenly, she had the feeling that a handful of stones had been placed in her tummy and had sunk to the bottom like bikes in a canal.

A flock of rose-ringed parakeets landed on a branch of a nearby elm tree. They were high enough from the ground not to have yet come to the attention of any of the cats or kittens. But, sensing the tension in the air even quite high up off the ground, they sat beside each other quietly in a row waiting to see what was going to happen next.

'Hey, look, everyone,' called out a very nasty voice. 'It's last year's loser, Catvinkle, and she's brought a dog!'

'That's Twinkiepaws!' Catvinkle whispered to Ula. 'Quick, pretend to be a cat who's disguised as a dog!'

All the cats turned to look. They saw Catvinkle with Ula who, being a dog, looked very much like a dog. They gasped.

'Gasp!'

'All right, everyone,' said Catvinkle in a louder voice. 'Now that you've gasped, you can all relax because this *isn't* a dog. It's a very famous cat disguised as a dog because she's on holiday and doesn't wish to be disturbed by a bunch of nosy kittens.'

'Sure looks like a dog to me!' said Twinkiepaws, strutting around as though she had already won this year's baby-shoe dancing competition and possibly next year's too.

Ula concentrated on Twinkiepaws for the first time. No taller than Catvinkle, Twinkiepaws was a little moving bag of muscles completely covered by cream fur. Her tail was the most eye-catching part of her. It was all primped and fluffy, extending wider than the widest part of her body, her tummy, and fanning out behind her almost like a peacock's tail, only instead of feathers there was fur. It was clear to Ula that Twinkiepaws was going to be a formidable opponent.

Catvinkle spoke in a haughty tone. 'You're going to choke on your own fur, Twinkiepaws, when you realise who it is you're calling a dog.'

'Who is it?'

'We can't tell you because then you'd know, and you're just the kind of cat this very famous New York singing sensation doesn't want to be bothered by,' said Catvinkle.

Twinkiepaws walked slowly around Ula. All the other cats were watching.

'Who are you?' she said.

'Don't be so rude, Twinkiepaws!' said Catvinkle.

Ula sat very still on the cool grass and remained silent.

'She can't tell you but I'm warning you, Twinkiepaws, you wouldn't want to be mean to a world-famous kitten singing sensation like

Ketzington . . . Oops! I told you who she is! I'm so sorry, Ketzington,' said Catvinkle to Ula, who was pretending to be Ketzington.

All the cats there at Kittens Anonymous gasped in shock. 'Gasp!'

All of them except Twinkiepaws.

'Catvinkle, I don't know what you think you're doing bringing a dog here, but this is not the wonderful Ketzington. This is a Dalmatian. You're crazy to bring a dog here, Catvinkle. We've come here for the National Kitten Baby-Shoe Dancing Competition, not to see what the cat dragged in.'

'You'll be sorry for treating our special visitor so rudely,' said Catvinkle.

There was much murmuring and muttering among the assembled cats and kittens. Some cats thought Ula might actually be Ketzington in disguise. Some cats thought she was definitely just a dog. Others weren't sure.

'Catvinkle's right,' said a wise old cat named Schrodinger. 'It's not wise to be so rude to someone who might turn out to be Ketzington.'

He strolled over to join them. 'Let's look at what we know. We know that Ketzington and the Snufflecats are due in Amsterdam at any moment. We would all agree it makes sense that a cat as famous as Ketzington would want to travel around in disguise so she wouldn't be constantly bothered for paw prints. And it makes sense that a successful singing star like Ketzington would be able to afford the best disguise any kitten could want. Of course, because we're cats, we're unlikely to bother a dog. So a famous cat wanting to be an anonymous kitten could indeed come to Kittens Anonymous dressed as a dog.'

Schrodinger stroked his whiskers with one paw thoughtfully. 'Anyway,' he continued, 'I've always thought that a cat we can't see can be both a live cat and not a live cat. And "not a live cat" could mean a live dog.'

'You really lost me with that last bit. Are we even *meant* to understand that?' asked Twinkiepaws.

'What you understand, Twinkiepaws, is entirely a matter for you,' said Schrodinger. He was so wise

that very few of the cats who gathered there knew what he meant, but he was used to this and spent many of his happiest hours having long conversations largely with himself.

'Oh, Schrodinger!' cried Twinkiepaws. 'You're not going to fall for this. Catvinkle is trying to trick all of us.'

'No, I'm not,' said Catvinkle.

'Yes, you are!' said Twinkiepaws.

'No, I'm not,' said Catvinkle.

'Yes, you are!' said Twinkiepaws.

'Kittens, please! Will we be any the wiser if you both just keep on saying the same thing?' asked Schrodinger.

'Not sure. Let's see,' said Catvinkle as Ula sat there quietly and very, very nervously. 'No, I'm *not* tricking.'

'Yes, you are!' said Twinkiepaws.

'No, I'm not,' said Catvinkle.

'Yes, you are!' said Twinkiepaws.

'Kittens, stop this!' said Schrodinger forcefully.

'Well, you were right, Schrodinger. It was fun but we're no wiser,' said Catvinkle.

'I'll tell you what,' said Twinkiepaws. 'I'll prove to you that this is not only *not* Ketzington, it's not a kitten at all. It's a dog!' And with that she jumped up in the air and landed hard on Ula's tail.

'Oww, oww!' howled Ula, in a voice that was so much like that of a dog that it seemed that Catvinkle's and Ula's attempt to convince everyone that they were looking at a famous cat disguised cleverly as a dog was not going to work.

CHAPTER 21

In her pain at having had her tail jumped on by Twinkiepaws – and her guilt at having let Catvinkle down – Ula ran away from all the cats at Kittens Anonymous.

In fact, she ran all the way out of Vondelpark and into the streets of Amsterdam, where she went looking for her cousin, hoping that Lobbus would give her some advice. She had never been in this situation before and didn't know what to do.

When she got to King's Square Street, Ula noticed something going on out the front of Friend's Herring Shop near where posters and banners were advertising the next day's first day of herring season celebrations.

There out the front of Friend's Herring Shop she saw her cousin, Lobbus the brave dog Lobbus, running around a table, followed by a llama, followed by Grayston.

'Lobbus, why is this big grey dog chasing me? Does he want to bite me?' called Roy Llama as he ran around the table.

'No, he wants to bite *me*,' called Lobbus, running around the table.

'I thought you said you *weren't* Lobbus,' said Grayston, running around the table after Lobbus with Roy Llama running between them, before adding, 'It's all so confusing.'

'Well,' said Lobbus, 'biting someone in the rump won't help anything.'

'I don't want to bite anyone,' said Grayston, still running. 'I only wanted to ask where Lobbus's cousin Ula was.'

'I'm right here. Leave my cousin Lobbus alone,' said Ula.

At hearing this, the three of them stopped running and crashed into each other, with Roy Llama in the middle.

Ula couldn't believe she had been so brave. She'd wanted to be brave but hadn't known she could be. She was still a bit scared but knew she had to do the right thing by her cousin Lobbus.

'Now look here,' said Lobbus, puffing and panting, 'you mustn't bite Ula either.'

'Why won't anyone listen to me?' said Grayston sadly, puffing just like Lobbus. 'I don't want to bite anyone.'

'So you're not cross about the rubber ball being given back to the children, Anja and Ferdi?' asked Ula.

'I have to admit I was angry before. But then my children spoke to me and, well, that's why I want to talk to you,' said Grayston.

'Really?' asked Lobbus.

'Yes,' said Grayston. 'My children are the most important things in the world to me. I love them so much, more than I can explain. Every morning

I wake up and look at them and I'm ready to burst with love for them.'

'That's very nice, Grayston. I didn't know you had that much love in you,' said Lobbus.

'Lobbus, do you think we'll be playing back-gammon soon?' asked Roy Llama.

'Shhh!' said Lobbus. 'Grayston, what does any of this have to do with my cousin Ula?'

'I was brought up to be a big scary grey dog and to bark at everything and to chase things that came near my house or my family,' said Grayston. 'But my children don't like my barking and my chasing and my running around.'

'I'm sure they like your running around,' said Ula.

'No, they want me to be more like you.'

'Like me?' said Ula, quite astonished.

'Yes, they want me to be happy and friendly, not grumpy and scary. Most of all, they want me to be the kind of dog that human children like Anja and Ferdi would want to play with,' Grayston said.

'So I came looking for Lobbus to help me find you, so you could teach me how to be that kind of dog,' he continued. 'I know it will be hard. I'm an old dog and you'd have to teach me some new tricks. But I'll try really hard, I promise. I didn't know where you lived so I thought I'd ask Lobbus. But I couldn't find him either – only this other Russian wolfhound who looks and sounds exactly like him and knows exactly how he thinks and feels about everything.'

'I will help you, Grayston. It would be my pleasure,' said Ula. 'And I know I could get Anja and Ferdi to come to play with your puppies. They always want to play with dogs and even a certain cat.'

Ula looked back in the direction of Vondelpark. 'But right now I have to help my friend Catvinkle. She's in trouble. She told all the other cats at Kittens Anonymous that I was a cat disguised as a dog. But they didn't believe her and now she's all alone with some terribly mean cats. I, too, came looking for advice from Lobbus.'

'Well, I don't know where Lobbus is,' said Grayston, 'but you can ask this dog who *looks* like

Lobbus for advice. He's a complete expert in Lobbus. It's almost like he *is* Lobbus. He knows what Lobbus would say about *any* matter under the sun – and probably what he would say at night too.'

Grayston paused. 'Hey! Wait a minute,' he said. 'Is your friend a *cat*?'

'Yes,' said Ula.

'Why are you wasting your time on a cat?' asked Grayston.

'I know this cat, Catvinkle,' said Lobbus. 'She is a good cat; loyal, brave and true. Okay, not true. Actually, she lies quite a lot. But still I think she's a good cat.'

'A good cat!' said Grayston. 'When I was growing up, no one ever told me there was such a thing as a *good* cat. This is a new world for me. Suddenly we're talking about cats and saying they're *good*!'

'Lobbus, what should I do?' Ula asked her cousin.

'You should go back to help your friend Catvinkle at this important time for her.'

'It's not Lobbus,' Grayston told Ula. 'It only looks and sounds like him.'

'But all the other cats there think I'm a dog,' said Ula to Lobbus.

'Tell them you *are* a dog. Admit it. Why not? You have nothing to be ashamed of. Dogs are wonderful. We're furry, fun, brave, good with children . . . well, most of us are.' Lobbus tried not to look at Grayston. 'Humans love us. Most animals think very highly of us. If these cats don't like dogs, it's their problem. As long as you're not boastful, you should be proud of who you are.'

Lobbus walked over to Ula. 'I'm going to whisper some words into your ear. Remember them, and if you get frightened just say them to yourself.'

Ula leaned in towards him and Lobbus whispered these words into her ear. 'Be strong and of good courage!'

'Be strong and of good courage! Be strong and of good courage!' Ula whispered to herself. 'I'll try to be strong and of good courage but . . .' She paused.

'But what, dear Ula?' asked Lobbus.

'Well,' said Ula, 'perhaps it would be a bit easier if some dogs could come to Vondelpark near to where the cats and kittens are having the baby-shoe dancing competition at Kittens Anonymous. It might help me to be strong and of good courage.'

'Baby-shoe dancing? Cats and kittens? Kittens Anonymous? I don't understand what the world's coming to,' said Grayston.

'I will try to muster up some support dogs just in case you need backup,' said Lobbus, 'but it may take a little time. A lot of dogs would still be at work now. You might have to take care of things on your own for a while. You can do it, Ula. I know you can. Remember,' Lobbus added, 'I've known you since you were a puppy just earning your spots, so I know you very well, dear cousin.'

Ula nodded, took a deep breath and turned around to go back to Vondelpark, to where Catvinkle was facing the disbelief of many of the other cats at Kittens Anonymous. Lobbus, Roy Llama and Grayston watched her as she went.

'Wow, that's one brave dog!' said Grayston.

'Yes,' said Lobbus, 'and she manages to be brave without scaring children. Do you see?'

'Yes, that's right,' said Grayston. 'She could be a great teacher for me.'

'Lobbus, do you think we'll be playing back-gammon soon?' asked Roy Llama.

'This is *not* Lobbus,' said Grayston. 'How many times do I have to tell you? It just *looks* like him.'

CHAPTER 22

When Ula got back to Vondelpark, Catvinkle was standing on a rock, still trying to convince the other cats that her friend really was the famous singing cat, Ketzington, disguised as a dog to avoid fans and unwanted attention.

'It's Ketzington, I tell you, and you made her run away. That's so rude of you!'

'Catvinkle,' asked Twinkiepaws, 'really, how stupid do you think we are?'

'Well, it varies from cat to cat, naturally,' said Catvinkle. 'You, I think, are *very* stupid. Schrodinger, not at all.'

Just as Catvinkle was saying this, she saw Ula

getting closer. Ula could tell that Catvinkle was nervous that all the other cats were going to find out for sure that Ula was really a dog, not a famous kitten singing star from New York. The rose-ringed parakeets with their bright green feathers sat as still as they could be on the branches high above, watching the whole thing.

Catvinkle didn't have much time. She had to get to Ula before her new friend did or said anything that might make things worse.

'Excuse me a moment, won't you?' she said to the crowd of waiting cats and kittens. 'I think Ketzington is coming back and she probably wants to speak to me privately. We're very close, you know.' Then she climbed down from the rock she had been standing on and started walking away from them towards Ketzington – who, of course, wasn't really Ketzington but Ula.

All the cats watched as the two friends stood talking quietly under a tree.

'Okay,' said Catvinkle almost in a whisper to Ula's ear, 'a lot of these cats definitely don't believe me.

But I think I've still got some of them thinking you're Ketzington. The important thing, Ulee, is to keep cool, look completely unafraid, and never, ever admit that you're not really Ketzington. We've got to keep this up. Don't take off your dog suit, whatever you do.'

'I'm not wearing a dog suit, I really *am* a dog. Remember?' said Ula.

'Oh yeah,' said Catvinkle, 'it gets so confusing, doesn't it?'

'Not if you tell the truth,' Ula began. She wanted to tell Catvinkle about Lobbus's suggestion that Ula should admit she was a dog.

But Catvinkle didn't seem to be listening. 'Whatever you do, Ulee, never, ever admit that you're really a dog.'

'Don't you want these cats and kittens to accept you for who you really are?' asked Ula.

'No, I'll be happy if they accept me for who I'm *pretending* to be. But thanks for asking,' said Catvinkle in a hurried whisper. She sounded as though she was very sure about this. 'Ulee, you don't really understand cats. Some of these cats can be very, very mean. They can make fun of you and try to make other kittens frightened to be your friend.'

'Why should other kittens be frightened to be your friend?'

'Because the *mean* cats will make them scared that if they're *my* friend they won't have any *other* cat friends.'

'But then couldn't you be friends with *those* cats?' asked Ula.

'Listen, Ulee, we don't have much time so I'll explain this as simply as I can. Everyone wants to be friends with the mean cats. That's just the way it is.'

'But if they're *mean*,' asked Ula, 'why would you want to be friends with them?'

'Because,' said Catvinkle, 'if you're friends with the mean cats, you think they won't be mean to *you* and that they will pick on someone else.'

'Who will they pick on?'

'I don't know. They're always changing it. Sometimes they pick on fluffy cats, sometimes on short-haired cats, sometimes on skinny cats who don't have enough to eat. Sometimes they pick on cats who've been forced by the incredible smell of yummy food to become tubby round the face and tummy areas. You just never know who they're going to be mean to.'

'That sounds awful,' said Ula.

'Yeah, it's tough being a cat. It's not all lying

around in a soft basket by the fire . . . Although, that *is* quite a lot of it.'

'I think you should be strong and of good courage,' said Ula.

'What?! Who told you that?'

'Oh, someone. I forget now,' said Ula.

'Was that someone your cousin, Lobbus the brave dog Lobbus?'

'Oh, yes, it *was* Lobbus. That's right,' said Ula, pretending that she had only just remembered.

'Well,' said Catvinkle, 'Lobbus probably doesn't know that many cats.'

'Oh, he has friends right throughout the animal world,' volunteered Ula.

'Ulee,' said Catvinkle, still very quietly, 'take a look at that bunch of cats over there staring at us.'

Ula looked over at them. Some were growing impatient. You could see it in their fur, which stood up a little bit from their bodies. The occasional tail was slightly raised too. And twitching!

'Hmmm . . . You're right. Some of them do look a bit mean, Catvinkle.'

'Right,' said Catvinkle. 'Trust me, I know them. Some of them are my oldest friends. So whatever you do, don't tell them the truth.'

Ula realised she had to make a decision. Should she listen to her new friend Catvinkle, a cat who really did know what cats can be like? Or should she follow the advice of her wise and loving cousin, Lobbus the brave dog Lobbus, who had met a lot of animals over the years and who had told her to be strong and of good courage? How would mean cats react to a dog with courage?

Catvinkle had started walking back to the waiting cats and kittens.

'Come on, Ulee,' she turned around to whisper.

What would Ula do?

CHAPTER 23

Ula walked back to Catvinkle and the other cats. Everybody, including the rose-ringed parakeets in the branches high above, was focused intently on her.

Then Ula did what might be the bravest thing she had ever done. She stood in the middle of a whole clowder of cats and kittens and told the truth about herself. Her tail was still hurting from Twinkiepaws jumping on it, and her heart was jumping about wildly inside her chest like freshly caught salmon in a net.

But she took a deep breath and repeated to herself, just in her head, the words Lobbus had given her as a gift. 'Be strong and of good courage. Be strong and of good courage.'

Then she spoke out loud.

'Hello, everyone. Some of you think I'm not really Ketzington the singing kitten disguised as a dog, and you're right. I'm not a kitten at all. As you might have guessed, I'm a dog. You may wish to gasp.'

'Gasp!' went almost every kitten there.

Ula continued. 'I'm a Dalmatian, to be precise. But the really important thing to tell you is that I'm Catvinkle's friend. I'm her *best* friend. She even lets me share her water bowl.'

'Gasp!' went almost every kitten there again.

'And because we're friends, I came along to give Catvinkle support and encouragement.'

Catvinkle smiled at all the other cats and kittens as she quickly made her way to Ula. 'Ulee, this isn't good,' she whispered to her. 'It's not going to help. Twinkiepaws is evil and she'll turn everyone against me. Tell them you're joking and that really you *are* Ketzington pretending to be a dog who confesses to not being Ketzington.'

Catvinkle backed away from Ula, smiling again at all the other cats.

But Ula went on. 'My name is Ula. I am Catvinkle's friend and I'm a dog. Catvinkle thought you wouldn't like it if she brought a dog here so she asked me to pretend to be Ketzington.'

Catvinkle slapped one of her front paws against her face. 'Ulee!' she whispered. 'What are you doing?!'

'You've never had a dog visit you at Kittens Anonymous, but maybe it's time to invite some,' continued Ula. 'Some dogs, not all, are terrific animals. Just as some cats, but not all, are terrific animals.'

'Kittens!' called Twinkiepaws. 'Surely you're not going to sit here and listen to a speech from a no-good dog?'

'Why am I no good?' asked Ula.

'You're a *dog*!' answered Twinkiepaws.

'Most other animals get on very well with us. Some even think very highly of us,' answered Ula. 'We've worked as guide dogs, watch dogs, fire

203

truck dogs, sniffer dogs, guard dogs, sheep dogs, sled dogs, rescue dogs, service dogs, and most importantly, therapy dogs bringing comfort to old, sick or sad people.'

'Oh boy! I think *I* need a therapy dog,' said Catvinkle quietly to herself.

'We've been doing all this for thousands of years,' Ula continued. 'We were among the first animals ever to travel in a rocket to outer space. We can also be extremely cute and have great senses of humour. Think of how many more friends you could have if you allowed dogs into your world. And anyway, are we really so different from cats? If you put a fresh water bowl in front of us, do we not drink? If you put a comfy wicker basket beside a warm fireplace, will we not crawl in and get snuggy?'

'I've had just about enough of this,' snapped Twinkiepaws. 'This is supposed to be the National Kitten Baby-Shoe Dancing Competition, not a lesson about dogs.'

Twinkiepaws glared at Catvinkle. 'For being a dog lover, Catvinkle shouldn't be allowed to compete in the competition. No one will want to be your friend anymore, Catvinkle.'

'Oh boy, Ulee. I *knew* this would happen,' said Catvinkle. 'Now I don't have any friends.'

'Yes, that's right,' said Twinkiepaws. She stood on a rock triumphantly and called to all the other cats and kittens. 'Let's not be her friend. Let's make it so that Catvinkle does not have one single friend.'

'But she *does* have a friend. She still has me,' said Ula.

Then Ula walked to the top of the rock and Twinkiepaws scampered down, not wanting to be so close to someone who was not only bigger than her but also a dog.

From the top of the rock, Ula called out, 'I'm sure some other friends of Catvinkle will make themselves known very soon.'

'Shhh, Ulee,' whispered Catvinkle from beside the rock. 'I don't think so. I don't think I have any other friends left now.'

'No, you're wrong there,' called a voice. 'You have Ula and you have me.' It was Lobbus, who had

just arrived and had heard nearly everything from behind a tree. 'I'm your friend, Catvinkle.'

There was another gasp from all the cats and kittens, who were amazed to see that Catvinkle had another friend who was a dog.

Ula had asked Lobbus to come, and here he was. He had come through for her and, in turn, he had come through for Catvinkle.

Then everyone heard another voice. 'Me too, I'm your friend, Catvinkle,' said Roy Llama, who decided now that it was time for him too to come out from behind the tree.

'Who are you?' Catvinkle said, a little confused.

'I'm Roy Llama,' said the llama who had come to help Lobbus who had come to help Ula who was there to help Catvinkle. The nervous white cat with the big red bow around her tail had all this help and it was all because of Ula.

Then another, younger voice was heard.

'I'm your friend, Catvinkle,' said Grace, one of Grayston's puppies, coming out from behind the tree.

'I'm your friend too, Catvinkle,' said Graham, standing beside his sister.

Now everyone could hear somebody pushing someone else out in front of the tree. It was Gram, the third puppy, pushing his dad, Grayston. When the cats and kittens saw big possibly scary Grayston they gasped again and backed away slightly.

'I'm coming, I'm coming,' whispered Grayston.

'I'm your friend, Catvinkle,' said the puppy, Gram. 'Dad, isn't there something *you* want to say?'

'But they're all *cats*!' said Grayston. 'I'd be talking to a whole clowder of cats.'

'Dad!!!' said Grace, Graham and Gram in unison, which means all at the same time.

'Okay!' said Grayston. 'Here goes . . .' He shook his head, scarcely able to believe what he was about to say. 'Gee, I must *really* love you kids.'

'Dad!' said Grace, Graham and Gram in unison again.

Grayston took a deep breath and said, 'I'm your friend too, Catvinkle.' His puppies all yelped excitedly when they heard this, which made Grayston feel much better about coming to the aid of a cat.

It seemed Catvinkle had a lot more friends than anyone had expected. This was such a surprise to Catvinkle, but even more of a surprise was the sudden return of the salty water to her eyes. This time, though, the salty water wasn't because she was sad or worried. It was because she was so moved with unexpected joy and gratitude by the support Ula had gathered for her from all these other animals. And to think, most of these animals were dogs!

Catvinkle realised that her new best friend, Ula, might well be more loving, more brave and more honest than any animal she had ever met. She understood now more than ever just how lucky she was that Mr Sabatini had invited Ula to live with them. Could there be a better best friend in all the world? Certainly not one with such great musk.

Catvinkle quickly rubbed the back of her front paws against her eyes so that no one would see the salty water. Now with the salty water almost entirely gone, she could clearly see all her new friends standing around her with their tails in the air, even Roy Llama's short one. She was far from alone. What would Twinkiepaws say to this?

'Don't pay any attention to them, my fellow felines,' cried Twinkiepaws. 'They're just a pack of dogs, mostly. And I don't even know what *that* one is!'

'Does she mean *me*?' asked Grayston, ready to be upset.

'I think she means *me*,' said Roy Llama.

'Oh, thank goodness,' said Grayston.

'I'm a llama, if you don't mind,' said Roy Llama to Twinkiepaws.

'What*ever*,' said Twinkiepaws. 'Talk to my tail 'cause my ears aren't listening.'

'*What* did she say?' Roy Llama asked Lobbus, but Twinkiepaws continued talking anyway.

'No self-respecting cat would hang out with a dog,' cried Twinkiepaws, trying to get the other cats all worked up. '*Would* you, kittens?!'

CHAPTER 24

From the back of the crowd came a voice that nobody expected yet all the cats seemed to recognise.

'I respect myself and *I* hang out with dogs . . . a lot.'

Everyone turned to see who was speaking. It was a very cool cat in dark sunglasses.

'Oh my goodness!' said Catvinkle. 'Are you . . .?'

'Yes, I am . . . Ketzington D. Kitten, at your service. These here are some of the Snufflecats.' Ketzington flicked an ear to indicate the cats standing beside her.

'You're the coolest cat in the world,' said Catvinkle.

'You're very kind to say that,' said Ketzington.

'But who's to say, really, who is the coolest? I once
met a tubby old tabby cat who lay on the linoleum
floor of a convenience store on a very hot summer's
night listening to some of his favourite blues music
on an old radio. A cheeky young mouse scurried
across the floor, teasing him, saying the tubby old
tabby cat would never catch him. That old tubby
tabby cat refused to move anything but his tail until
his favourite song, "Dust My Tail", was over. Then
he leaned over, caught the mouse with one paw,

put it in his mouth, walked over to the front door and spat the mouse out right onto the street. Now that's one cool cat!'

'Ketzington, we think you're the greatest, coolest cat ever!' gushed Twinkiepaws.

Ketzington frowned. 'Aren't you the cat who doesn't want kittens to hang out with dogs? I heard what you were saying. One of my best friends back in New York is a rapping dog, name of Snout. You ever heard of him?'

'No, sorry, I don't listen to that kind of music,' said Twinkiepaws.

'What kind of music is *that* kind of music?' asked Ketzington.

'Dog . . . music,' said Twinkiepaws nervously.

'You need to open your ears and your heart. Twinkiepaws, is it?' said Ketzington.

'Yes.'

'We're all *mammals*, aren't we, Twinkiepaws?' asked Ketzington.

'Well . . . yes.'

Twinkiepaws felt something was changing.

It wasn't the wind but it felt a bit like it, as though she was all of a sudden a bit colder than she had been a moment earlier.

Ketzington had let everyone know that back in New York she had friends who were dogs. In fact, she was quite open to friendship with dogs anywhere. Twinkiepaws could see the other cats thinking about this, thinking about dogs in a new way for the very first time. 'Yes,' they were thinking, 'we have to admit, from time to time one *did* hear about a cat here or there, getting along well with a dog, even if the story was told in whispers through whiskers that fanned the scandalous words away from the kitten who said them as soon as the words were in the air. How long can we pretend not to have heard those stories, at least once or twice? Maybe it happens more often than we care to say?'

Twinkiepaws could see such thoughts on the faces of these cats. Their eyes were slightly narrowed, the fur on their foreheads was slightly scrunched up and crinkly, and their heads were moving slowly from side to side, a sure sign of kitten-thinking.

They were thinking further, 'Well then, if it *does* happen from time to time and if Ketzington likes dogs, maybe *I* could like some of them. Maybe *I* should try to see dogs differently too?'

This new thinking of a few of the other cats was working in favour of Catvinkle. Twinkiepaws could sense the change – maybe not in every cat, but in quite a few.

Now it felt as though not only was the wind changing direction, but it was blowing directly on Twinkiepaw's tail, and she felt unexpectedly colder in the area of her rump.

Just then Schrodinger spoke up to invite Ketzington to judge the National Kitten Baby-Shoe Dancing Competition. All the other cats thought it was a good idea.

Ketzington agreed immediately, since she was already very familiar with baby-shoe dancing. Cats and kittens in New York had been doing it in their clubs downtown and on Ketzington Avenue for years.

'My parents actually met at a baby-shoe dancing competition,' said Ketzington. 'It was at a club called

Studio Fifty Paws, a place where the coolest cats in town used to go to dance and purr, sip a little cream and wait for the sun to come up,' she explained. 'So I grew up with baby-shoe dancing, always had a soft spot for it. I've always thought kitten paws look very elegant in baby shoes.'

'They certainly do, they certainly do,' said Twinkiepaws, who was in a very big hurry to make Ketzington like her after she had said the wrong thing about dog music.

So everyone, including Ula, Lobbus, Grayston and his puppies, along with Roy Llama, made their way to the Vondelpark bandstand down on the lake. None of the kittens wanted to miss it. Cats were huddled together all the way along the bridge that led to the bandstand. Some of them stood on top of other cats and kittens and some of *them* stood on top of still *other* cats and kittens, forming a small mountain of cats.

Those who couldn't get a spot on the bridge sat on the grass on the bank of the lake as close as they could get to the bandstand where the competition was going to take place.

Ketzington was surprised to learn that this year there were only two contestants. All the cats pretended they too were surprised by this.

Catvinkle explained the reason for the lack of contestants to Ula. 'After Twinkiepaws won the competition last year,' Catvinkle whispered, 'the other cats were too frightened to compete against her. You've seen how mean she can be.'

'But you're not too scared, are you, Catvinkle? You're brave. You're standing up to her,' Ula whispered back.

'Thanks, Ulee, but now I have to win – and with everyone looking on and with Ketzington as the judge, the pressure is on me like never before.'

Twinkiepaws was jumping up and down, stretching from side to side and furling and unfurling her tail as though it was a flag. She looked very confident as she took the stage.

'Okay, well, I guess you only need two contestants, even in a national competition?' said Ketzington.

Twinkiepaws put on her baby shoes. They were pink with big yellow bows. She looked over at

Catvinkle and Ula with a very mean face, stuck out her tongue very quickly, and then turned back to Ketzington with the smile of an angel who had just come down from the sky in the form of a cat.

Twinkiepaws was indeed a very good baby-shoe dancer and she had carefully worked out a complicated dance that was ready to go. She had spent a lot of time practising.

But because she was so desperate to win – more than ever given that Ketzington was the judge and that her only opponent was that dog-loving Catvinkle – she decided not to do the dance she had been rehearsing for weeks.

Instead she decided to take a very big chance with something new. In an attempt to make Ketzington choose her as the winner, she sang one of Ketzington's songs as she danced. She moved her tail slowly to the left and then to the right, picking up speed as she went.

But because she had never practised her dance routine to this song, because she didn't know all the words and because she kept looking at Ketzington every few seconds, she wasn't very good at all. She realised things were not going well and just thinking this made them go even worse.

Instead of concentrating on her dance moves and her singing, she imagined how Ketzington must be seeing her – as the mean cat who was ruining one of Ketzington's own songs. Twinkiepaws was forgetting the words and then making them up. It really was not going at all well for Twinkiepaws. Her dance moves were all out of time with the beat of the song.

She thought she needed urgently to do something that would really stand out, something quite spectacular. So she tried a backflip. Her bottom paws went over her head with her tail following, but the problem was that her right bottom paw got stuck in her ear. She quickly pulled it out and tried not to let anyone see how much it hurt. But because this backflip hadn't gone very well she thought she'd better try to do another one. This one was even worse. On her second backflip she fell completely off the stage. In fact, she fell right off the bandstand and into the lake. She dog paddled her way sheepishly back to the island with the bandstand and clambered back up to the stage. She was soaking wet and the drips made a puddle where she stood.

'Gasp!' went everyone.

Except Roy Llama, who whispered to Lobbus, 'I thought we were going to play backgammon.'

'I *meant* that second backflip, you know, the one that might have *seemed* as though I were falling and then tumbling into the lake,' Twinkiepaws said. But no one seemed to believe her and anyway, whether she meant it or not, it looked horrible.

Twinkiepaws could tell that no one was very impressed with her dance or her song, and she scurried down the ramp from the bandstand to the grassy bank with her tail between her legs. This had been one of the worst days she could remember, and she had a good memory.

Then it was Catvinkle's turn. On her way to the stage she went to Ula and, in front of all the other cats, she sniffed the back of Ula's coat for its musky goodness.

'Thanks, Ulee,' she whispered to her best friend.

On the stage, Catvinkle stood on her hind legs with her tail in the air, her front paws raised and bent at the elbow. She put one bottom paw in the right baby shoe and one bottom paw in the left.

With her eyes closed, Catvinkle counted softly to herself, 'One, two, three,' and began to dance.

She swung her rump to the left and then to the right and back again with her tail going in the opposite direction. Then she called out in a strange voice that Ula had heard before.

'Ah-huh, ching ching, Ah-huh,
    Ah-huh, ting ting, Ah-huh.
Ah-huh, ching ching, Ah-huh,
    Ah-huh, ting ting, Ah-huh.
I'm a winking cat, name of Catvinkle.
I'm a winking cat, name of Catvinkle.
Ah-huh, ching ching, Ah-huh,
    Ah-huh, ting ting, Ah-huh.
Ah-huh, ching ching, Ah-huh,

Ah-huh, ting ting, Ah-huh.
I wiggle from the middle,
    it's a riddle how I twiddle.
Ah-huh, ching ching, Ah-huh,
    Ah-huh, ting ting, Ah-huh.
Ah-huh, ching ching, Ah-huh,
    Ah-huh, ting ting, Ah-huh.
I'm a winking cat, name of Catvinkle.
I'm a winking cat, name of Catvinkle.
Ah-huh, ching ching, Ah-huh,
    Ah-huh, ting ting, Ah-huh.
Ah-huh, ching ching, Ah-huh,
    Ah-huh, ting ting, Ah-huh.'

Ketzington loved both Catvinkle's song and her special baby-shoe dance. No one was at all surprised when Ketzington announced that Catvinkle was the winner.

CHAPTER 25

The very next day all the animals went to celebrate the first day of herring season at Friend's Herring Shop on King's Square Street. The humans were so excited by the herring that they didn't notice the procession of animals. At the front of the animal procession was Catvinkle, standing on top of Ula's back.

Catvinkle took her first bite of her first herring of the season and was so happy, she purred.

'You'd better eat it all, Catvinkle. You didn't eat much yesterday,' said Ula.

'Oh, Ulee, it is such a lovely piece of herring! It's as if my birthday – which is soon – has come to visit my mouth!'

'Is your birthday coming up soon?' asked Ula.

'Very soon. How did you know?' said Catvinkle. 'Do all dogs celebrate my birthday or will it just be you?'

Just then Anja and Ferdi arrived with their aunt to try some herring. When they saw Catvinkle and Ula they rushed to hug them.

Grace, Graham and Gram jumped up and down on the spot near the children, hoping to be patted. In the busy crowd the children didn't see the puppies until Ula introduced all three of them. Now the puppies would have Anja and Ferdi to play with. Grayston stood back watching proudly.

'Do you want to play backgammon after the herring?' Lobbus asked Roy Llama.

'No, not really,' said Roy Llama. 'I'm sick of backgammon.'

Then, on a stage not too far away, at a pitch only cats, kittens and dogs could hear, Ketzington and the Snufflecats started to play a concert.

Catvinkle was so excited by so many things that her paws became all tingly. She had won the

National Kitten Baby-Shoe Dancing Competition the day before and her birthday was coming up. She was thinking that maybe, for a birthday treat, Ula could ask Lobbus to introduce them to the new koala that was coming to the zoo. Lobbus had friends in all different parts of the animal world so he would probably know someone who knew the koala.

She was also excited to be eating her first herring of the season, which tasted especially good only one day after she'd won the National Kitten Baby-Shoe Dancing Competition.

In the distance she could hear the music of Ketzington and the Snufflecats, and it was great. The day before, Ketzington had invited Catvinkle to visit her in New York, and to hang out with her and the Snufflecats.

It was all so exciting that her tail started spinning and, with her big red bow acting like the propeller on a helicopter, she started to fly.

Ula looked up at her friend hovering in the air. 'Catvinkle, you're flying again!'

'Oops,' said Catvinkle. She flopped down onto Ula's back and sniffed Ula's musk. 'Don't tell anyone.'

'I won't,' said Ula. 'Do you think it's our secret?'

'I do, Ulee, I do!'

Mr Sabatini saw the whole thing and was very glad his two friends got on so well. But he wasn't going to tell anyone about the flying. He knew how to keep a secret too.

The very next morning, Mr Sabatini came into Catvinkle's room, so that he could bring Catvinkle, in her basket, into the bathroom so he could talk to her while he shaved. He smiled when he saw her sleeping with Ula beside her.

Ula opened one eye. It seemed to Mr Sabatini that Ula winked at him.

Mr Sabatini whispered to them both, 'I'm going to have a shave before I go out to breakfast. Anyone want to come with me?'

First Ula flicked her tail against the ground once, and then Catvinkle flicked her tail against the padding of her soft basket.

Mr Sabatini took this to mean 'yes' so he picked up Catvinkle's basket and Ula followed them to the bathroom. As they made their way down the hall, Mr Sabatini saw that a pair of baby shoes was lying on the floor. They were crocheted light blue with a dark blue zig-zag pattern, and on each shoe there was one brown button the colour of a tortoise's shell.

'Hey, did you see those baby shoes on the floor in the hallway?' Mr Sabatini asked them both. 'I wonder who owns them. I'll have to try to remember which baby came in when someone wanted a haircut so that I can return the baby shoes to their rightful owner. We should probably give them back, don't you think?'

At this, Ula's ears pricked up, and just as suddenly Catvinkle sat up in her basket. Ula trotted out of Mr Sabatini's bathroom towards the hallway and then Catvinkle jumped out of her basket and followed her as fast as her padding paws could take her.

Mr Sabatini followed. He wasn't as fast as his two furry friends but he got to the hallway just in time to see Ula pick up one of the baby shoes in her mouth and Catvinkle, close behind, pick up the other one. He followed them back to their room, the one that Catvinkle used to have all to herself.

Mr Sabatini looked around the room but there was no sign of the baby shoes anywhere. All he could see was Ula pretending to be asleep in front of the fire, with Catvinkle on top of her also pretending to be asleep. Mr Sabatini realised that the baby shoes must be hidden underneath them both.

'Oh well,' said Mr Sabatini, 'I guess that if you love something enough, you'd better keep it close by.'

There was a little flick of Ula's tail on the soft red carpet. Then came a little flick of Catvinkle's tail on Ula as she buried her nose in Ula's fur. It seemed everyone was in perfect agreement.

The author wishes to thank Liv Perlman Handfield,
who first heard a version of this story when she was four
and who would thereafter periodically remind the author
to write it down over the ensuing thirteen years.

ABOUT THE AUTHOR

ELLIOT PERLMAN is the bestselling author of a number of novels and a story collection for adults, which have been translated into many languages, won literary awards and adapted for film and television. When his niece was young, he began to invent stories for her. Now that Elliot has two children of his own, he decided it was time to write down those stories. The result is his first book for children, *The Adventures of Catvinkle*.